Thwarting Harold.

Fiona J Roberts

Chapter 1

It was a Thursday, which meant it was night school

evening. Iris had become a devotee of the many courses on

offer at the local college, which was fifteen minutes, walk

from her home. So far, she had studied photography,

computer coding, that had been tricky and remained

unmastered, and now she had moved onto conversational Spanish.

This latest one had not been a good idea. None of them had really. Repeating Spanish phrases, knowing that she would likely never get to the country, was making her more depressed. They were an excuse to get out of the house for a couple of hours a week. A short time to relieve her of the tedium of her life. Some precious moments away from her husband.

Iris Joan Thomas, nee Noble, was twenty-eight, petite and blonde. Well, blonde after the highlights, a bit mousey underneath. For some reason, she had thought it was a good idea to get married at the age of twenty-three. It was an escape from the claustrophobia of her family home, she supposed. As an adopted child, her older parents had smothered her with affection. There was appreciation for what they had done and she loved them, but she needed to get away. She had more autonomy now, no one fussing over her, but, instead, she had endless nights watching documentaries on television and monosyllabic conversations.

Iris knew that she was adopted from a young age. No traumatising revelation in her teenage years. Her real mother, whatever that meant, had died weeks after her birth. No one had stepped forward to claim her, so she went to the Noble family. They were kind, but, old fashioned people. Fine when she was a child, but stifling when she got to her teens.

Mike had seemed such a catch. An older man with his own home and a good job. He made her laugh and, although he was ten years her senior, he never talked down to her. She had been in love, but what was it now? The meals out and the weekends away had gradually disappeared. He seemed exasperated with her at times, their sex life, was non-existent. Three years into the marriage, they were only going through the motions.

Night school had saved her from going insane. The first course, photography, had been populated mainly by men. There had been interest and offers from a couple of them, but she had rejected them because she was married. Had those overtures come now, two years further on, she might have said yes.

The latest class was full of older ladies and gentlemen who were learning Spanish for when they went to stay in their villas. Iris was at least twenty years younger than any of them. Mike was ten years older than her and she wasn't looking to increase the age gap. Still, everyone was pleasant and she wasn't doing too bad with the language.

Mike had asked, once, whether she was okay walking home in the dark at 8.30pm. Having been assured that she was okay, he never enquired again. Most of her journey was on a, well lit, main road and she was not the nervous type. Cars flitted by and she walked along repeating Spanish sentences in her head.

It was not too cold, so the pace was slow. Ambling along, delaying her return home, where she would make a cup of tea and then watch the television, maybe read a book or the newspaper. There needed to be more to life than this. Muttering some Spanish swear words, Iris sighed and trudged on.

Two youths were loitering on the pavement ahead. Iris was busy thinking about the latest lesson and when she found her path blocked, it came as a surprise. They weren't that old, these boys in front of her. Fourteen or fifteen, she thought. They were in the youth uniform of track suit bottoms and hoodies. The trainers they were wearing seemed rather nice in comparison to the rest of their clothes.

The, slightly, taller one was the first to speak.

"Give us your phone."

The lad had made an assumption. Iris didn't have her phone on her and now she would have to explain this to the young man who, she had just noticed, was waving a small knife at her. Keep calm, she told herself.

"I haven't got my phone with me. It's at home."

"What's in the bag?"

"My books. I'm learning Spanish."

She might as well have been speaking Spanish. The boys looked at each other and the knife waver shrugged at his mate. It was the smaller ones turn to threaten.

"What about your purse. Cards and money and stuff."

Thug number two also had a knife and had taken a couple of steps towards her.

Iris had to decide what to do and she didn't have long to think about it. The muggers were only kids. Hopefully, they wouldn't actually use those knives, but it was best not to antagonise them. They weren't getting her bank cards, Iris decided. There was about twenty-five pounds in the purse and they would have to be happy with that. She took the bag off of her shoulder and began searching inside.

What a lot of crap she carried around with her. She could see three lipsticks, tissues, gloves, keys, various receipts, a packet of paracetamol and, finally what she was looking for. Looking back up at the muggers, it became apparent that she had missed something. They were backing away, clasping each other's arms.

They weren't looking at her any more. Something far more fascinating was behind her. No, not fascinating, terrifying.

"What's the matter?" Iris asked.

"Fuck that."

They turned and ran. Not a jog or a fast walk. It was as if they were competing in the Olympics. Their expensive trainers were being used for their real purpose for once. It was at this point that Iris felt the shiver. Whoever, whatever, was behind her, had not made a sound. No footsteps to herald their approach and no movement that she could discern. The fear that had gripped the boys, was now creeping up on her.

There was nothing that could make her look behind to see what was there. Choosing the quick walk instead of the manic sprint, Iris set off and put a good thirty feet between her and the scary thing, before she risked a glance back. All that she saw was a swirl of mist. Her footsteps rang out as she picked up the pace again. The last few yards were covered at a jog.

Deep breath, key in the lock and then she was inside the house. She ran a trembling hand through her hair and took a moment to compose herself. When she walked into the living room, Mike's eyes didn't leave the television, but he acknowledged her arrival.

"Hi. Okay?"

"Yes, fine. I'll put the kettle on."

Mike was a financial controller at a large engineering company. A man of figures and maths. A man who pointed out all the inconsistencies in whatever film or programme they were watching. He was tall and dark, with a touch of grey at his temples. Handsome? He had a kind face, she thought, and very blue eyes, which she loved, but he was pretty ordinary, really. Iris stood in the kitchen thinking about her encounter with the thing. It would likely invite ridicule, but she would tell him.

"I've just had the strangest experience. Some louts tried to mug me, but they were frightened away by…well I don't know what it was. Something that scared them and made them run off. When I looked around, I couldn't see anything other than a patch of mist which was dispersing."

Mike took the offered cup of tea and then studied Iris.

"Say that again."

Iris repeated her story and then waited as he mulled it over.

"Some lads tried to mug you?"

"Yes, but that's not the point."

"No, no. I mean that is worrying, but something scared them, you say."

"They kind of staggered backwards, mouths open and then turned and sprinted away."

"And there was no one behind or near you?"

"No one. The road was quiet. I know I was being mugged, but I heard no footsteps, noise or voices. The boys can't have heard anything either, or they would have legged it before they did."

"Where was this?"

"Just around the corner, by the post box."

"Maybe you shouldn't walk back from night school any more. I can come and pick you up."

The response from Mike had been interesting. He had spent the rest of the evening frowning. He had glanced at her quite often, giving a small smile. When she headed up to bed, he had told her not to worry about the evening's events. Iris found it hard to sleep though. What had made the, would be, muggers flee like their lives depended on it?

Chapter 2

The incident still occupied her thoughts the next morning. Mike liked to get to the office early and had been out of the door before she sipped on her first cup of coffee. The words exchanged had been the usual, have a good day, see you later, but Mike had stroked her shoulder as he left. That, too, was interesting.

There was not much physical contact between them now. Mostly any touching was accidental. Getting in each other's way in the kitchen, or a brush of fingers when food was dished out. Iris had nearly shrunk away when he reached towards her. How bad was that. His fingers on her back had felt alien, but comforting. She had nearly got mugged and he was worried about her.

Work for her was behind the counter of the local post office. Some of the customers sorely tried her patience, but she never let it show. She knew many of the locals and the older people made a beeline for her because she would smile and help. Alongside her was Wendy. A few years older than her and a little more abrupt. They got on well and met up for drinks, sometimes, of an evening.

Iris shared some of her troubles with Wendy. She shared a bit more with her best friend, Mel. Neither of them was aware of how miserable she really was. They saw a woman who had a mortgage free home, a kind and, well off partner, and an easy life. All of those things were true, but she was bored and it felt wrong to moan about her lot. Others had way more problems than her.

Wendy was divorced and had two teenage kids who were lazy and uncommunicative. They sat in their rooms gaming, surrounded by dirty plates and mugs. Her best friend Mel was single and in search of a husband. Each man she met was the one. None of them lasted long. Still, it meant that there was a, never ending supply of stories about disastrous dates and awkward encounters.

Iris had decided that the scary thing was a ghost. It was the only explanation she could come up with. The silence of the approach and the terror of the boys who saw it, could not mean anything else. As far as she was aware, there were no ninjas in the area, so this was the best option. She would not tell Wendy, but she would tell Mel. During her lunch hour, she made a call.

"Hi Mel, can you talk?"

"Yes. The boss is God knows where and I am enjoying a quiet couple of hours."

"I needed to tell you about last night."

"Ooh, sounds fascinating."

"It was, but not in the way that you think."

"Shame."

"I was nearly mugged walking home from college, but a ghost came to my rescue."

"What?"

"Two boys tried to rob me. I was looking in my bag for my purse to give them money and then they were looking behind me, frightened out of their wits and then running for their lives."

"It was a ghost? What did it look like."

"Ah, well, I didn't actually see it. I had the creeps myself. Walked away quickly and when I looked back, there was just a wisp of mist. It was swirling off in a weird way."

"Not much evidence, Iris."

"There was no sound of anyone approaching, so what scared the lads? I didn't hear anything leave afterwards, either. It was pretty scary and I thought, ghost. What else could it be? There was no fog or mist that night either. Just that small patch which drifted away as I looked at it."

"Well, it's a good story. Had you had a couple of drinks last night?"

"No, I was at Spanish class. Completely sober."

"I'm not convinced, but it sounds a bit strange if nothing else. Did you tell Mike?"

"Yes. He didn't just dismiss it, like I thought he would. You know how practical and logical he is."

"If Mike believed you, then I guess I have to, as well."

"I didn't say he believed me."

Iris had been surprised that Mike had listened and not disagreed. At the very least, she thought he might have suggested they go back to the scene of the crime so that he could look for evidence. He liked evidence. Instead, he had discussed the encounter and then thought about it. At least, that's what she assumed from the look on his face. The pat on the shoulder came to mind again. Maybe he thought that she was losing her marbles.

That night, Iris cooked a proper dinner. Guilty of buying ready meals and slapping them into the microwave, she made a toad in the hole, which was one of Mike's favourites. He had not dismissed her story and if he could make the effort to improve things, so could she. Would there be any comment on the food? She wasn't holding her breath.

They sat at the table and ate in silence. So far, so normal. Mike placed his knife and fork on the plate and looked at Iris. Not looked, studied.

"You okay, Mike?"

"Yes. I really enjoyed dinner. You haven't made that in a long while."

"No. Fancied something home cooked."

"I'm glad you did."

Silence and then Iris picked up the plates. They had been closer to really talking in that moment than they had been for months. Maybe years. Once again, they both backed away and the chance was gone.

Chapter 3

"THANK YOU, MRS FERGUSON."

Wendy rolled her eyes at Iris.

"She can't help being deaf." Iris explained.

"No, but she could turn her hearing aid up. You're practically a saint the way you deal with the old people."

"I just think, that could be my grandma or grandad."

"I know. You're quite right Iris, but you're still a saint. I'll go and make us a cuppa. Your throat must be sore after all that shouting."

A smile was exchanged and Iris took advantage of the lack of customers and stretched before checking her phone. She was trying to arrange a night out with Mel, but was, temporarily, of less importance to the present Mr Right. When the first flush of infatuation was over, she would try again.

The thought she kept having, was that she should share more about her feelings with Mel. Most of the time, when they got together, she deflected and then listened to her friend's tales of the latest dating disaster. Mel would find the right man at some point. Until then, Iris would enjoy the crazy stories.

The confession of her, less than ideal marriage had been rehearsed in her head a number of times. The last couple of days had made everything more difficult. Mike seemed to be taking a bit more notice of her. Was it wishful thinking, or had they really got a little closer? Mel was not the best person to ask for relationship advice, but Iris needed a sympathetic ear and she would provide that.

A few weeks passed and Iris and Mike continued to talk and care a little more about each other. At moments when she was lost in her thoughts, the events of the ghostly encounter were replayed. An explanation eluded her. Mark it down as a mystery. An amusing story to tell friends.

Iris made her way to the car park after finishing work. As usual, the path through the park was her route. It had been raining during the day and mud was spread across the path. Looking at her nice suede boots, Iris studied the area to see if there was a crossing point that would do no damage. She could take a running jump, but that might spell further trouble.

A breeze stirred and the autumn leaves began to dance. A swirl of red and gold. The foliage formed a column, as if caught in a whirlwind and then deposited itself across the mud forming a carpet. Walter Raleigh, his cloak and a puddle came to mind. As the final leaf fell, a wisp of mist drifted away. It was happening again.

The icy chill ran down her spine. This spirit seemed to be some sort of guardian angel, but why did she feel unsettled and scared? Iris took the run and jump, preferring to avoid the carpet of leaves. Back home, she awaited Mike's return from work, so that she could update him on the latest weird episode.

"Hi Mike."

"You alright?"

"I think I've had another ghostly encounter."

Mike sank into a chair, shaking his head.

"Tell me about it." he said quietly.

"I was walking through the park and there was mud on the path. I was worried about getting my suede boots dirty and then a wind whipped up from nowhere. A load of leaves was blown into the air. They twirled around and then formed a carpet over the mud. The mist, like before, was there and then drifted away. It covered the mud for me."

"It wasn't just a fluke. The leaves landing on the mud like that."

"No. They placed themselves across the mud. Nowhere else."

"A kindly spirit then. It seems to be looking after you."

Mike mumbled the response and Iris sank into the chair opposite him. The ghost might be friendly, but neither of them were happy about it.

"It still gives me the creeps."

"You don't like the idea of something following you around?"

"No. It makes me feel uncomfortable."

Dinner was eaten in silence. They glanced at each other, exchanged small tight smiles and then carried on. Maybe the spirit was sitting at the table with them, quashing any chance of conversation.

When Mike left home the next morning, he said goodbye and then added "Take care". Kind words which seemed so ominous, said as they were in a low tone with a laser focussed stare into her eyes.

Chapter 4

Iris didn't walk through the park that morning. Following the road made her journey a little longer, but it was worth it for the peace of mind. As soon as she got a chance, she messaged Mel. A meet up and a couple of drinks were desperately needed. The buzz of her phone heralded a reply.

"I can do Friday evening. The Dog and Duck at 7.30."

Iris punched the air and replied in the affirmative.

Mel and her had met at senior school. Her friend was a tall, voluptuous brunette. There was never a problem attracting men, but standards were high and, after a few dates, they were usually rejected. A couple of the boyfriends had lasted for a few months, but then something happened and they were dropped, too.

Iris hadn't met all of Mel's dates. They weren't around long enough. She had met a few and they were of a type. Attractive, a bit cheeky and not ready to settle down. "You have a talent for choosing the wrong men." she had told her friend. Mel just shrugged and then repeated the same mistakes again.

The days dragged and finally, it was the appointed day. When she left home there was another "Take care" from Mike, followed by a hug as she went out of the door.

Mel was already there and a glass of wine was sat on the table waiting for her. Iris grabbed the glass, took a big swig and then sat down before saying hello.

"You look like you needed that." Mel noted.

"Bloody right. Are you okay?"

"Yes, fine. Come on spill the beans."

"Give me a minute. First of all, tell me about this Ian chap. How's it going?"

"Well, I don't want to jinx it, but he is turning out to be relatively normal and rather nice."

"So, he doesn't eat like a pig?"

"No."

"Or call his mother every half hour?"

"No."

"Or criticise what you're wearing?"

"No. If he has a strange foible, it has not revealed itself yet. I don't feel anxious either. Talking about anxiety…"

"I don't even know where to start. You remember the ghost thing a few weeks ago? Something similar has happened again. Before I get to that, I really ought to talk about Mike."

Iris took a deep breath.

"For, I don't know, the last two years I suppose, Mike and I have drifted apart. We don't really communicate. We talk about shopping and paying bills. What laundry needs doing. Stuff like that. He watches documentaries and I go to night school. That's it. That's our lives."

Mel rooted around in her bag, found a tissue and handed it to Iris, whose eyes were misting as she spoke.

"Everyone thinks I'm so lucky. Nice man, plenty of money, lovely home, but it means nothing if you are unhappy. I feel so ungrateful, but I'm miserable. We don't go out anywhere or do anything. What's the point of having money if you don't enjoy it. I don't know how to talk about it with Mike. How stupid is that."

"It's not stupid. Relationships are hard. I should know."

They both managed a smile at that.

"Anyway. Then the thing with the ghost happened. I don't know why, but it made us talk a bit. Not enough, but it's a start. He listened to me when I told him about it and didn't take the mickey. Then I cooked him a nice dinner and that helped, too. I know they all seem like tiny things, but somethings happening."

"I can't tell from your tone whether you're pleased that something positive is happening, or what."

"Confused, I suppose. We've practically ignored each other for the last two years and now it's all change. I'm reading too much into it, I think. Noting that my husband is talking to me and checking I'm alright. Those things shouldn't be remarkable. I thought I was done with him. I supposed that we would stumble on for, maybe, another year and then split up. Now, feelings are returning. I don't want this to be just a reaction to the mugging which will disappear in a couple of weeks.

"I've been trying to protect myself. Convince myself that I'm fine with my marriage going kaput. The feelings were still there, though, and this has brought them all out again. I have to hope that Mike feels the same and that we can work this out."

"You said there had been another ghost thing."

"Yes. It will sound crazy, but it, the ghost, whipped up a load of leaves and laid them on mud. I'd been worried about walking through it with my suede boots on. I saw the mist again and it made me feel scared. I told Mike and now he keeps fussing and telling me to take care. I'm so confused."

They sat in silence for a moment. Mel looked like she was going to speak a few times, but couldn't quite find the words.

"I know, I know. A lot for you to take in. Sorry I haven't told you any of this before. About me and Mike, I mean. I was hoping things would get better and I wouldn't have to tell you how unhappy I'd been."

"Oh, Iris. You can tell me anything. You need to talk to Mike. If things are looking more hopeful for you two, you should seize the moment. He's showing he cares, but it takes two of you to keep it going."

"You're right, of course. Easier said than done."

A man bumped into their table and then grinned at them.

"Alright Ladies."

Iris and Mel tried to ignore him and carry on talking.

"I said, alright ladies."

Mel glared at him.

"We're fine, now go away."

The drunk's lip curled and he was about to speak again, probably some ripe language would be headed their way, when he threw beer all down himself. It was like an actor in a comedy skit. As he lifted the beer, his elbow flipped up and he tipped it all down his front. He was more surprised at this turn of events than anyone else. He whirled around looking for someone to blame.

"Who did that? Who shoved my arm?"

Mel gasped and grabbed Iris's arm.

A member of the bar staff came over and steered him towards the exit. The man, looking startled, put up no resistance.

"Did you see that?" Mel asked.

"His arm moved like he'd been jostled. Then there was mist."

"Shit, Iris. What the hell is going on."

Mel's hand was shaking as she reached for her drink.

"I'm going to the bar. More wine?"

"God, yes."

They didn't stay at the pub for long after that. Mel hugged Iris like they would never see each other again when they got outside.

"Message me to say you got home alright."

Mel was fussing about her, too.

Back home, Iris walked into the lounge where Mike was watching TV. He took one look at her and got up from his chair. Seconds later, she was sobbing and he was holding her tight.

"The ghost again?"

"Yes. Mel saw it, as well. Not the ghost, I've never actually seen it, but she saw what it did. It knocked the arm of an annoying drunk, who then spilled beer all down himself. There was mist afterwards. That's three times now. This is not my imagination. Something is really happening."

"I'll go and make tea, or do you want wine or something?"

"More wine, I think. I need to get a bit drunk, so that I can forget this thing for a while and get some sleep."

Mike opened a bottle and poured them both generous glasses. Iris sat on the sofa next to him and they huddled close together.

"Have a drink, get some sleep and then we'll talk about this in the morning."

They held each other tight all night. Iris didn't get much sleep. The ghostly incidents kept replaying in her mind. The look of terror on Mel's face after what happened in the pub, kept appearing in her mind, too. It was good to know that Mel had seen it and that she wasn't going mad, but scary that her suspicions had been confirmed.

The message Mel had sent, after receiving the text that Iris was home safely, was unsettling, as well. "Take care."

Chapter 5

Mike was unnerved to say the least. His wife had imagined that she had seen a ghost. Then she had, allegedly, seen it again. Her best friend Mel had seen it, as well, now. No more pretending that this wasn't happening. A ghost was following Iris and making its presence known.

Talk about being wrenched out of his inertia. Mike would have to start facing the various problems which he was, currently, doing a good job of avoiding. Iris was freaked out, and possibly in danger, and he would have to step into the fray. These events had made him realise how much he loved his wife and how stupid his attitude had been.

There were reasons, he had told himself, for retreating from Iris. The decision on whether to have children was a major factor that had caused him endless turmoil. This was the moment to tackle these subjects and get them sorted. It was a lot harder to do in practice, though. He couldn't seem to find the right words.

Mike's thoughts had turned to a conversation with his mother many years before.

"I need to talk to you, Mike. I'm turning the television off, because you need to listen."

"It's a bit late to do the birds and the bees talk, mum. I'm twenty-one."

"Yes, very funny. Seriously, Mike, sit down and pay attention. You know I've been looking into the Thomas family history, since Becky. Well, I've found out some interesting and frightening things. I want to tell you about them and pass on the paperwork that I've collected. There are documents, photographs and notes that I've made."

"You make it sound as if something is going to happen to you. You're not ill, are you?"

"No, but you never know what might occur."

Some of what was said had hit home, but a lot of it had been shoved to the back of his mind and marked, things I don't want to believe. Now was the time to reconsider what he had been told. It was also time to locate the box into which all of his mother's research had been put.

The box had been dutifully carried from his old family home, via various rentals and flats, to his current home. Mike couldn't get rid of it. He remembered his mother's words and had felt that it was necessary to keep it. Somewhere, up in the loft, it nestled awaiting his attention. A trip into the past might supply the answers to the present troubles.

It had been forced on Mike, but he must capitalise on this opportunity. He had been gifted the chance to talk to Iris properly, about their marriage and their lives. He began to rehearse in his head what he would say. Finding the box and going through the contents would remind him of the story he was told by his mother and then they could find a way forward.

Lurking in the back of his mind was a worry. There had been a warning from his mother. There was bad news in that box. He managed to recall the basis of the conversation and it was something to do with a curse. As a practical man, he would normally dismiss any such thing, but recent events made him rather anxious.

A new panic was taking hold. Yes, he and Iris could have a, much needed talk, but he was about to unload a whole lot of information on her. Things he had never spoken about and that would provoke reactions that would be difficult. Anger, sorrow and, hopefully, forgiveness were likely. Mike wanted to ignore it all, as was his usual way of coping, but this time the box and the story were coming out.

Chapter 6

"Are you going to your parents this morning?"

Mike placed a mug of tea in front of a, bleary eyed, Iris. He didn't look much better himself. Weary and frowning he slumped into the seat opposite her.

"Yes. You not coming with me then?"

"No. Send my love to your folks. I've got some stuff to do. I'm going up into the loft to get something."

Iris's face made an inquiry, but no explanation was supplied.

Sue and Tony were in their late sixties. They lived in a small, neat bungalow, ten minutes, walk from where Iris lived. Retired, they tended their immaculate garden, went out once a week to their favourite café for lunch, spent a week in a caravan for their summer holiday and for the first hour of each day, they drank coffee and did the crosswords in the papers.

Iris had found everything about them cloying and predictable as a teenager, but now, she loved the solid ordinariness of their lives. She would go into the house and her parents would hug her, offer her tea, ask if she needed anything to eat and how she was. The same routine, in the recent turmoil of her life, was comforting.

"Hi Mum, Dad."

"Iris. Let me get you some tea. How are you? Are you hungry?"

She smiled at them and gave them another hug. They looked bemused for a second and then reverted to normal.

"I'm in the middle of pruning the roses. Chat with your mum and I'll be back in shortly."

Her dad always made an excuse to disappear so that the women could talk.

"How's Mike?"

"He's fine. He said he wants to get something from the loft. Not sure what, he didn't say. He sends his love."

"And how are you?"

"Fine. Saw Mel last night which was good."

There was no way on earth that Iris was going to tell her parents about the events of the previous few weeks. Talk of ghosts would completely blow their minds. The last thing she wanted to do was cause them any worry.

"You look a bit tired, darling."

"Had a sleepless night. I was grateful to be coming here this morning. A bit of TLC is just what I need. I didn't want to end up in the loft with Mike and all the spiders. Come on mum. Get the biscuits out."

The sound of the biscuit tin opening brought Tony in from the garden. Peeling off his gardening gloves he selected a chocolate one. He took a big bite and grinned in response to Sue's tutting.

"Come and have a tour of the garden."

Tony made the suggestion, which meant it was time for Iris to spend a bit of time with him. They wandered out to the garden and Iris peered at the greenfly, all two of them, and listened to plans he had for jet washing the patio.

"You alright Chicken?"

She had always been, Chicken to him. The name was not appreciated at first, but it had grown on her.

"Yes, just a bit tired."

"If you need anything, you only have to ask."

Iris made an excuse and went back into the house. Looking at his kind and concerned face for a moment longer would have made her cry.

It was time to go home. Big hugs for mum and dad and then she walked off, turning to wave a couple of times. She went into her house and was met by a scene of carnage. Boxes, suitcases and bin bags littered the hallway.

"Hi. I thought while I was looking for something, I'd sort out all the stuff up there. A fair amount we can get rid of and a couple of finds. That lovely old leather suitcase and a couple of vases which look like antiques."

"Did you find what you were originally looking for?"

"Oh, yes. We'll have some lunch and then I'll show you."

The tone of Mike's voice changed as he spoke. One minute upbeat, the next morose. Iris wanted to know what he had found and didn't want to know what he had found. A sense of foreboding lingered throughout their lunch and after clearing up in the kitchen they went into the lounge where a large wooden box waited on the coffee table.

Iris sat on the edge of the sofa. A dramatic pause and then Mike lifted the lid. A smaller box was stuffed in the corner and the rest of the contents appeared to be documents and notebooks.

"I have never opened this box before. My mum gave it to me before the accident. She talked about what was in it, but I've forgotten a lot of it. She was quite manic about it and I've tried to put it to the back of my mind. We need to go through everything in there and I think it might help."

"Help with what?" Iris' voice trembled as she spoke.

"The ghost."

Somehow, she knew that would be the answer.

Chapter 7

Tony and Sue were nearing their forties. Unable to have children of their own, they had decided to adopt. They saw the baby girl, just a few weeks old, and they knew that she was the one for them. Iris didn't even have a name at that point. The tragic story of the death of her mother, was told to them and they were even more determined to give this orphan a chance in life.

Like most parents, they learned on the job. Tears, theirs, and frustration turned to delight as they got the hang of it all. Not everything was straightforward, that's life. The teenage years were particularly fraught. Old fashioned parents and a girl of thirteen, was a volatile mix.

"We have to get a bit more with it, Tony."

"What do you mean?"

"I know teenagers are difficult, but we are talking a completely different language to Iris. Pop bands and clothes. Computers, as well. We need to learn more about things and then we might be able to have a conversation where she doesn't roll her eyes and stomp off."

"I know you're right, but I'm not looking forward to our re-education."

"Then it will be boys."

"Oh, Lord, save me from that."

"This is just a blip. She says the odd hurtful thing about being adopted, now, but it's all those hormones making her lash out."

"Yes. If we can weather the next few years, hopefully, we'll get the old Iris back."

"We will."

They did. Iris appreciated everything that Tony and Sue did for her and found ways to tell or show them how valued they were.

The adoption had never really been an issue. Iris had known since she was a small child that they weren't her biological parents. She had asked a few questions, but nothing complicated or tough. The enquiries came in those teenage years, when she was challenging their authority, and then they subsided. Should they tell her everything that they knew about her early life, or stay silent on the topic? If she wanted to know more, surely, she would ask.

Sue felt a bit guilty about not discussing it more with Iris and Tony said that they shouldn't rock the boat. Conversations on the theme preoccupied them for a while, but eventually, they too, managed to put it aside.

Their daughter's marriage to Mike, so clever and dependable, had brought them great joy. They weren't getting any younger and he would be there to care for her when they were gone.

"Iris didn't look very well, today."

"Don't worry yourself, Sue. She said she had not slept well, that's all."

"What if it's more than that?"

"If it was more than that, she would tell us. We brought her up well and if she needs anything, she will come to us."

"You're right. She's got Mike, too. At least, I think she has."

"You sense trouble in paradise, as well?"

"For some time. I've been waiting for her to say something, but she hasn't. Do you think I should ask her about it when she visits next time?"

"No. Let her make the move. The last thing that she wants is interfering old people."

"We're her parents."

"We're also, if we poke our noses in, interfering old people."

"Right. That garden won't look after itself. Unless you are making another cuppa and letting me have another chocolate biscuit, I'm off."

"Do some work, Tony, and then you might get that biscuit."

Chapter 8

Mike's parents had died shortly after his twenty-first birthday. He had told Iris that they had been in a car accident, which was true, but had omitted a few details. Their deaths would be just one part of an incredible story. Before they even got to those revelations, there were other things to discuss.

"Before we start on the box, I need to…explain some things. First, and most important, is that I love you Iris. I might not have shown it much lately, but it's true. You are kind, putting up with those old customers in the post office, and patient. You're calm, as well. Nothing bothers you that much. At least that's what I've always wanted to believe. I made that an excuse for not trying to sort out whatever problems we were having."

Iris was getting worried now.

"Things have been hanging over me. I've been caught in a dilemma. This ghost thing has made me get my act together. No more burying my head in the sand."

"You're worrying me, Mike."

"I'm sorry. I never wanted to face any of this. I've hardly believed it myself, but now I know it's all true. The ghost is one of my ancestors. My great, great uncle, I think."

Iris sat back in her seat. The ghost was one of Mike's relations. How did he know this and why did she now feel even more scared?

"His name was Harold Thomas. My mum started looking into the family history and the paperwork in the box relates to what she found out. She began her investigation after my sister died."

"Hang on a minute. I didn't know you had a sister, My God, Mike. Why wouldn't you tell me about that. What happened to her?"

"Becky was only six when she died. She was two years younger than me. I remember her, what she looked like, her laugh, but a lot of things have been forgotten. She had dark hair like me. The blue eyes, too. There was a bit of that annoying little sister stuff, but mostly we got on well."

There was a pause as he was lost in thought for a minute.

"She was in the garden and a swarm of bees landed on her. She panicked, like any child would, and was stung hundreds of times. Turns out that she had an allergy. Just one sting would have probably killed her, but with so many, she didn't stand a chance."

"Did you see it happen?"

"No, thank God. Mum did though. Saw it all play out in a few moments through the kitchen window. Dad and I were at a football match. We came home to an ambulance and neighbours crying in the street. I didn't think about it at the time, so much was happening, but dad mentioned the Thomas family curse and I think mum got obsessed with the idea of it."

"The Thomas family curse?"

"Yes, there was some story passed down that the family were cursed. Why they had come to that conclusion had been lost over the years. I suppose mum needed an explanation or a distraction from the grief. She was determined to get to the bottom of it. She spent years going over old records and archives. Dad wasn't too happy about it, but he let her get on with it. I don't think he imagined that she would find any evidence."

"She found something."

"Yes. A whole story. Some of it came from older relatives of dad. They managed to give some clues and relate some incidents. There were wild tales about deaths in the family. Mum got copies of death certificates and newspaper clippings and found that a lot of the things had actually happened. I remember her telling me some of it, but I've forgotten a lot of the detail. At the time it all sounded a bit mad. Mum had been a bit unhinged since Becky's death, but she wanted to tell me. I listened to her and then shrugged it off. I think there are notes in here that she made. It will help me get the story straight. Let's get the things out of the box and then we can see what she discovered."

Iris peered into the box. She was drawn to the small box within it. It looked like it might contain jewellery. Reaching in, she grabbed it and pulled it out. Opening it up, she found a ruby ring inside. She showed Mike and he nodded.

"Ah yes. It's coming back to me now."

The items in the box had been put into neat piles which were held together with string. There was a stack of notes on lined paper. Death certificates had been bound together. An album contained newspaper clippings and another had photographs of Mike's ancestors. Iris looked at the pictures. They were interesting, but also a delaying tactic. She was not sure that she wanted to know what Mike's mum had discovered.

The ring drew her attention again. Part of her wanted to try it on, but she resisted. Iris turned it over in her hand. Mike was watching her and she switched her focus to him.

"I think that ring belonged to Harold's wife, Edith."

"I know that something bad happened to her."

"What makes you say that?"

"It kind of fits the narrative."

It did fit the narrative, but Iris believed it without really knowing why. They sat in silence for a while. Mike was reading the notes and was leafing through the death certificates. After a while he moved onto the newspaper clippings. The tension of watching him read and his changing expressions, ever more alarmed, had given her a headache.

A story was emerging and it was bizarre and frightening. Mike shook his head from time to time and then put the notes aside as he massaged his temples.

"I've read the first part. The least bizarre part of the story. Let's start with that and then I'll get the rest of it sorted in my head."

Chapter 9

As Mike told the story, from his mother's notes, Iris looked at the photos of Harold and Edith and could almost see their tale unfold. The dour looking Harold, unsmiling as he stood next to the pale, waif that was his wife.

Harold and Edith had a son, Bertie. It had been a difficult birth. Edith was small and sickly and she had taken to her bed for a month after he was born. Harold had taken on many of the duties of looking after the boy. Edith held Bertie and fed him from a bottle, she had been unable to breast feed, but Harold was the one that got up in the night, changed him and cared with him.

His brother was getting married and they were invited to the wedding. The rest of the Thomas family had not seen Bertie or Edith since his birth, so there was considerable pressure for them to attend. Harold persuaded his wife to go, the offer of a new dress helped, and Bertie got a new outfit, too.

There was never a direct link to the wedding. No one had seemed ill, but Harold insisted that the flu, that took Edith two weeks later, had been caught there. He had been forced to make her attend, so it wasn't his fault. The blame lay with his family for passing on the disease.

Harold and Bertie never saw the other members of the Thomas family again. They were the villains and he cut off all contact. Bertie grew up without a mother. Harold lived without a wife, paying fees for nannies and helpers instead. He never married again. A bitter man with no spare money, a young son and an idealised memory of his wife, wasn't a good prospect.

He lived a short life. At forty-two, he died in his sleep. His life had not got any better over the years. Bertie had joined the army at the first opportunity, to get away from a house full of negativity and acrimony. In 1917, at the age of eighteen, he had enlisted. War had broken out a few years earlier and he had gone to do his duty, but never came back. Killed almost as soon as he arrived at the front.

"He didn't take any action against his family while he was alive. Legend has it, that he started his vendetta from beyond the grave." Mike ended the story.

"In the pictures, Edith looked pale and sickly. If anyone was going to succumb to the flu, it was going to be her."

"I suppose he was overcome with grief and that made him need someone to blame."

"Or, he was annoyed at the inconvenience of losing a wife when he had a baby."

"Either way, he was furious and took his anger with him."

"So, for whatever reason, he blamed the Thomas's and, somehow, in spirit form, he has taken his revenge. A bit of a tall tale, I think. How exactly has he done that?"

"This is where the family legend was born. Lots of unusual deaths. Rumour and gossip kept the story going. It wasn't until my mother looked into it, that it began to look like there may be some truth to it."

"This is where the newspaper clippings and the death certificates come in."

"Yes, and I have mum's notes. I'll read the next section and then we can carry on with it."

Iris was beginning to get uncomfortable. She had left Mike to examine the documents. His mother had compiled them and she thought he should be the one to go through them. What on earth was coming next.

Had the ghostly Harold not made his presence known, Iris would have found the whole thing preposterous. Also, the spirit had helped her on each occasion it had appeared. How was that a curse? Something was coming which would explain the fear in Mike's eyes.

Mike was surrounded by the contents of the box. He had got some paper and was now making his own notes. Amongst the scribblings were family trees. The starting points for these were Harold and his siblings. He had an older brother, Reginald and then a younger brother Henry, followed by the youngest, a sister called Elizabeth.

In his usual methodical way, he was putting all the facts together before presenting them to Iris. She didn't mind. He was learning all the details and it was hard for him to take in. Better to receive the story in a coherent way than try to put it together from odd snippets. She could wait.

There was a small pile of things which had referred to the story of Harold's life. Whilst Mike was busy scribbling, Iris picked through those things. The death certificates for him, his wife and son, written in copperplate on faded, yellowing paper, did not give much information. A newspaper column included Bertie's name in a list of deceased soldiers. Not much evidence that they had ever lived.

Iris wondered if any of the Thomas family had gone to Harold's funeral. Was he one of those sad cases, where there was only a vicar stood at his graveside. Another reason for him to hate his relatives. As for Bertie, had there even been a body to bury? Maybe Penny, Mike's mum had found out about that. She grabbed the notes and scanned them.

Sighing, she put the notes down. Mike looked up and waited for her to tell him what she had just read.

"I was thinking about Harold. How much hate he must have had to, as you say, take it to the grave. It seems that Bertie died in the war, but his body never made it home.

His father didn't even have a funeral for him. His wife, then his son, you can understand why he was broken."

"Not everyone who has a tragedy in their life carries on a vendetta from beyond the grave."

"True. Have you sorted through everything yet?"

"Nearly. What we need is a takeaway and, more importantly, some wine."

"What do you fancy?"

"Chinese, I think. A few things that we can pick at."

"Leave it with me. I'll grab a bottle, as well."

Iris found the takeaway menu, opened a bottle of wine and poured two glasses. She took a gulp from one of them and then topped it up. Extra fortification was required. Mike's glass was put on the coffee table and half an hour later, when the food arrived, it remained untouched. He was lost in the paperwork spread out in front of him.

Chapter 10

Harold was tucked into the middle of his family. His older brother Reginald was a thoughtful child who was academic. The bright one. His younger brother Henry was the one that strangers stopped and cooed over. His blue eyes and wavy dark hair made him an attractive boy and people were drawn to him. Elizabeth was the baby and was fussed over by everyone.

As the children played in the house, or the garden, Harold was often on the periphery. He couldn't seem to find his place among the Thomas family. He was shorter than Reginald and not as good looking as Henry. He wasn't as clever as his older brother or as funny as his younger. There was no way to compete with Elizabeth, the only girl.

School was an escape of sorts. Harold could cope with the lessons, although he was never top of the class. He was happy to be away from the constant competition at home. The teasing and the practical jokes were never funny to him. Grin and bear it was the only way, because any reaction made things worse.

To be honest, Harold would sometimes think, his life wasn't too bad. His parents were, mostly, kind, although punishments were harsh when they were dished out. The family weren't poor, so there was enough food, decent clothes and they were getting an education. Those thoughts never quite dispelled his idea that he was the least favoured of the four Thomas children.

The horseplay of their younger years, became less as they got older. It was no fun trying to drag Harold into some game and having him complain or sulk. Being left to his own devices was a bonus for Harold. He longed to be free from his siblings. He studied hard at school, hoping to get a good job and, therefore, an opportunity to go out and make a successful life.

Part of his new life would be a family of his own. Harold would treat all of his children the same. He would make sure that they were kind to each other, no teasing or name calling. His wife would, of course, be beautiful and gracious. They would take a stroll on a Sunday afternoon and his family and neighbours would be jealous of his perfect life.

Harold often imagined his brothers and sister deferring to him. They would comment how handsome his family were and ask his advice on a range of subjects. They would want to know who his tailor was, why his children were so well behaved and how his wife remained so youthful and luminous. All he had to do was find this remarkable girl.

A distinct lack of interest from the opposite sex was proving to be an impediment to his ambitions. Reginald was already walking out with a, fine looking girl called Elspeth. Henry had women swooning whenever he glanced their way. Elizabeth was a pretty young girl and her future would be secured by a good marriage. Who was going to look at Harold?

He had a job. It was a clerical position, so at least he wouldn't have to get his hands dirty. Harold went off to work each day wearing a suit and a hat. Once he got a few paces from his front door, he strode out more confidently. People would see a man heading to an important job, he hoped. The moustache he had grown helped him to look older, which helped.

It was whilst walking down the road, that Harold first saw Edith. A delicate beauty, flanked by her parents. She took tiny steps, which made her look as if she was gliding along the street. He was mesmerised. The day on which she looked straight at him, Harold was in a good mood. Work colleagues were puzzled, but pleased at his change in demeanour. Sadly, it didn't last.

Money in his pocket, a lovely girl taking notice of him, Harold's life was looking better. He didn't share his excitement with his siblings, they would find some way to tease him about it. He would show them. He would marry the beautiful girl. He would have a family that he was proud of. He would succeed.

Chapter 11

Mike read, made notes, crossed things out, ripped up pages and huffed a lot. Iris ate most of the food and drank most of the wine and then went to bed, leaving him to it. He had said goodnight and waved a hand when she left the room and she was happy with that.

She was still awake when he crawled into bed beside her in the early hours of the morning. Iris lay there debating whether to start a conversation with Mike, but soft snoring indicated that he was already asleep. What would the morning bring?

Bacon sandwiches, cups of tea and a pile of paper were on the table. Iris looked at Mike and he nodded. The story was about to begin.

"Great, Great, uncle Harold had three siblings. Older brother Reginald, I'm from his line and I'll deal with him last, Henry was two years younger than him and Elizabeth was the youngest. As we know, Harold's son died in the war and that is where his line ends. So, I'll turn to Henry and his children."

Mike produced the appropriate photos from a file and placed them in front of Iris.

"This is Henry and Mabel."

"I can see some similarities between Harold and Henry. They definitely had a different taste in women. Edith was tiny and Mabel looks a bit more robust. A bit of a battle axe, I think."

The picture showed a slim man with the obligatory moustache and a large stern woman. A small hat was balanced on her large head. Mike frowned disapprovingly at her observation.

"This picture shows them after she had given birth to three children. I'll try to find an earlier one. Here we go. A, slimmer and less careworn woman in this one."

"Yes. She's even smiling. Henry's a bit of a looker, as well. That wavy rakish hair and a twinkle in his eye. I wonder what happened to make her look so dour. I suspect that you are about to tell me."

"Henry and Mabel had three children. Their first child was named after his father, Henry, two years later came Louise

and then a gap of four years to Peter. At the age of twelve
Henry died. This was sad, though wouldn't be particularly
noteworthy were it not for the manner of his death. The
family were watching a St George's day parade when a
horse bolted and ran into the crowd. The only person
injured in the incident was young Henry, who died."

Mike sat back in his chair. Iris could not quite get the
significance of the event.

"It was an accident."

"Yes, it was. However, have a look at this newspaper
article, that my mother found,"

*The annual St. George's Day parade ended in tragedy,
when a young boy, Henry Thomas, was trampled to death
by a horse. Members of the crowd scattered in panic as the
animal suddenly took fright and galloped towards the
spectators. Remarkably, the boy was the only one hurt in
the incident.*

A Mr Benson, who was watching the parade, stated that.

"It was the strangest thing. The horse was calm one moment and then went mad. It headed into the crowd, knocking the boy to the ground. It then turned around and stamped on him. It was almost as though it was doing it deliberately."

A doctor was called, but the boy had already died by the time he attended. Mr Henry Thomas senior and his wife Mabel have two other children.

Iris, put the newspaper clipping down and shuddered.

"That was gruesome. Especially as the family were probably watching it happen. I can understand Mabel's expression now. Poor woman."

Mike shuffled his papers, cleared his throat and then went on with the tale.

"Both Louise and Peter married. Louise had one child named Robert. Her husband died in the war. Robert married in his thirties, but there were no children. That's the end of that line. Let's move onto Peter."

More photographs appeared and Iris inspected them. Louise and her husband, dressed in uniform, and the young Robert. Just one of so many who had gone off to fight for his country and had never come home. Peter and his wife were actually smiling in their picture. She found herself smiling back at them. Mike still looked glum and she began to worry what was coming next.

"Peter and Grace had four children. The eldest boy was named Henry after his grandfather and the brother who had died. Then come three girls. Alice, Mary and Juliet. It was Mary who was the unlucky one this time."

Mike did the air quotes as he said, unlucky. Iris adjusted her seating position and took a sip of cold tea. She was ready for the next bit.

"The family were going on a trip to the seaside. Travelling by train, they were still heading for their seats when it pulled away. As they passed one of the doors, it flew open and Mary fell out and died."

A moments silence as they both contemplated the death.

"Mum managed to speak to Juliet about it. She was around eighty, but has died now. She said that the door opened and it was as if Mary was sucked out of the door in a puff of smoke. She could still picture it happening all those years later."

"In a puff of smoke?"

"Yes. An odd turn of phrase, I thought."

Iris got up and put the kettle on. A puff of smoke. A swirl of mist. Hot tea steamed on the table and the conversation resumed.

"Juliet seems to have said a few weird things. She spoke about Mary's guardian angel letting her down. Mum tried to get her to clarify what she meant, but Juliet did a fair bit of rambling. The idea she got was that Mary had led a charmed life up to then. A couple of near misses. Something about a car and being stopped from crossing a road. Sounds familiar doesn't it."

This was all too much. Iris burst into tears.

Chapter 12

There was a manic chopping of vegetables as Iris prepared for their roast dinner. Mike had stopped at the point she started crying. A break was needed from the grim stories about his relatives. He would resume later, he said, as it felt necessary to relate them all. She understood that somehow.

Two of Mike's relatives had died, so far and there were more branches of the family to be explored. His sister and the bees. That was another one. What about his parents and their car crash? Iris couldn't bring herself to ask about that yet.

Marital indifference hadn't interrupted the tradition of the Sunday meal. They still made the effort every week. The chicken was moist, the roast potatoes were crispy and the vegetables were perfectly seasoned. Why did it all taste like sawdust? There were leftovers, unheard of for a roast dinner. Time to resume their journey into the Thomas family's history.

"You ready?"

"Yes, Mike. Let's get it over with."

"Okay, so Mary has died, that leaves Henry, Alice and Juliet. They all grew up and married. Juliet was childless,

Henry had two children, a son and a daughter and Alice had three kids. We'll look at Alice's children now."

"Oh, no."

"I know it's tough, but I've got to keep going. Alice's children were Kenneth, Joyce and Shirley. It was Shirley, at the age of nine, who fell, hit her head and drowned in a shallow puddle. That thing they say, you can drown in two inches of water, seems it's true. She was walking home from school, down a lane behind their house. When she was ten minutes late, Kenneth and Joyce were sent out to look for her and found her dead."

As he spoke, Mike slid a couple of photos across the table. Three kids with grubby faces mugged for the camera. The smallest girl was Shirley. A pretty little thing about five years old. Half way through her life.

"It's not just the kids dying, that is bad enough, but the rest of the family suffer trauma, too. Seeing them die or finding their body."

"Like mum and Becky"

"Yes." Iris whispered.

"Edward and Jean, Henry's children, escaped an early death and it was Jean's child that was the next to die. A daughter, Debbie, was walking through the town when part of a building collapsed. Bricks rained down on the pavement. No one was hit except her. Another miracle escape, for other people who just happened to be passing by and a death for one of the Thomas family."

"Bloody hell."

"Mum spoke to Debbie's brother, Brian. He spoke about his sister's ghost. He said that the family used to tease her about it. They thought she was just an imaginative child. Instead of a pretend friend, she had a ghost."

"Harold again."

"Some members of the family didn't want to talk to mum when they knew she wanted to discuss the curse. She thought that either they didn't believe it, or were frightened of bringing the bad luck to them."

"Is there much more of this?"

"A fair bit. Let's get Elizabeth out of the way. That sounds awful, but you know what I mean. She had two children. Maurice and Abigail. It was young Abigail who died, aged nine. The cause of death was said to be poisoning. She died in 1920, so they didn't have the technology to say what had killed her, but they suspected it was mushrooms."

"Why did they think that?"

"A rare type, Deadly Webcap, was found in the family garden. It took her some time to die. Mum looked it up and it makes you vomit and eventually destroys your kidneys."

"So, the family got to watch her die in agony."

"Precisely."

"And Maurice?"

"He emigrated to Australia. Mum only got a bit of information. One of his daughters died, but there are no details."

"Trampled by sheep, probably."

They exchanged tight smiles.

"I'll talk about Reginald, my direct relative next. Mum seems to have given up with the other brothers and sisters lines at some point. It must have been depressing and increasingly worrying, learning about all the strange deaths. Add into that, the talk of ghosts and she must have been freaked out."

"Is there anything in the notes about her thoughts?"

"No. it's mostly facts and figures. A bit of speculation when she couldn't find details, but, although I don't remember everything, her fear was what stuck with me when she talked about it."

"I bet you thought she was crazy."

"I was confused. Since Becky, she had been off kilter. I thought this was another aspect of that. I was looking at her face, full of anguish, and only half hearing the words. I got the gist of it, the curse etc., but I just pushed it down and tried not to think about it. Some aspects of what she was saying got through. Things kind of haunted me for a long time."

Iris reached over and took Mike's hand. His smile was followed by sadness. This was all bringing back the memories of his sister and parents. It must be hard for him.

"Do you want to talk about it?"

"Not right now. I will do. Let me get to the end of the story and then what I want to say will all make sense."

"Okay."

"I'm going to move on to Reginald. Give me a minute and I'll get the paperwork together."

Iris stacked the dishwasher, washed up a couple of things, wiped everything clean and put the kettle on. Mike was lost in his project again. Shuffling pieces of paper and straightening them into a neat pile. He peeled off the top sheet and placed it on the table ready for her inspection. She sat down, took a deep breath and then nodded to say she was ready.

Chapter 13

Harold Thomas had married young.

He had always felt rather ordinary. A man of average height and average intelligence. Not brave, not good looking, never destined to be rich and powerful. The dainty girl who caught his eye was a neighbour. He only saw her occasionally, but on meeting her parents, he would enquire after her.

Edith was frail. Her father and mother described her as either resting, or under the weather. She would sometimes wave to Harold as he walked along the street, from her bedroom window. A pale face and a shy smile that seemed impossibly romantic to him. At last, he plucked up the courage to ask if he could call on her.

Trying not to scratch as his over starched shirt scraped against his skin, Harold sat motionless as Edith was ushered into the room. Her dress was ivory, almost matching her skin, and she moved with tiny steps. She looked like an angel. Her parents watched as their daughter and Harold sipped tea.

Finally, Harold found his voice.

"I'm so pleased to get the chance to speak with you, Miss Hills."

"And, I you, Harold. Please call me Edith.

"I hope you are well today?"

"Yes. I'm tired sometimes, but today I have been fine. I was looking forward to seeing you."

"It would be nice to go for a walk, if we get suitable weather. Would you like that, Edith?"

Her eyes went to her parents and they nodded their assent.

"Yes. That would be lovely."

Did he really know Edith before he made a proposal of marriage? Not really. Was he rushing into marriage when he was too young to know his own mind? Very likely. Did he feel that no one else would want him? Definitely.

The courtship had been swift and perfunctory. Harold couldn't wait to parade the lovely Edith in front of his family. They would see her, wealthy, parents, too. He would surely move up in their esteem when they saw how good his life was going to be. The life he had imagined was within his grasp.

The ceremony was small. Harold invited only his parents and three siblings. Edith was an only child, so her parents and her uncle and his family, were the only family, on her side, to attend. The sound in the, almost, empty church echoed as they said their vows. A meal at a local restaurant, paid for by the bride's parents was the only celebration.

Mr and Mrs Harold Thomas took the train to the seaside, where they stayed in a hotel for two nights, before returning to start their married life. Living with Edith's parents, at first, was not ideal, but a gift of money from them meant that they were able to move out within a few months. Proper married life was about to start.

Chapter 14

"Oh, a family tree. This will make things easier to follow. This must have taken you ages, Mike."

"I kept getting the spacing wrong and then had to start again. I needed to do it, though, so that I could understand it all myself. This is my side of the family and I wanted a record of my ancestors. I didn't do Reginald and Elspeth's other children's lines because it got a bit complicated."

"I know people die, but just on that one page I can see one, two, three, children that died. More gruesome accidents, I suppose."

"Yes. Lucille was found hanged. A bow around her neck that had caught on a

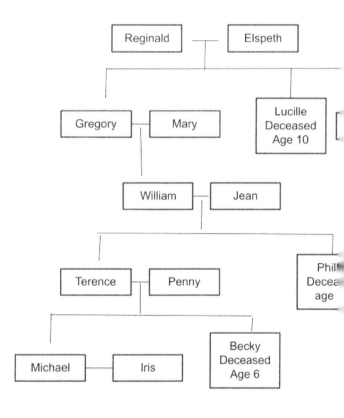

door handle. Phillip was crushed when a load of logs fell off of a lorry. There was some compensation from the company for that death. I don't expect Harold was happy with it. You know about Becky and the bees."

"Were there more casualties in, let me see, Charles and David's families?"

"Yes, but like mum, I was getting depressed by it all and gave up on recording those as well."

"All children. The worst thing anyone can do is take away someone's kids."

"There were some adult deaths, too."

"Oh, my God."

"Juliet's husband was hit on the head by a ball, playing cricket and died. A cousin in Australia died at the age of thirty-six when a cat tripped him up and he went head first through a shop window. And then there was my parents."

Iris looked up from the family tree in front of her. Mike's eyes were shining with unshed tears.

"You said it was a car accident."

"It was. The circumstances were very odd. A cow jumped over a fence onto the road. The car swerved to avoid it and hit a tree, head on."

"Oh, Mike."

"Mum had told me about the curse a few weeks before. She never mentioned seeing the ghost, but I suspect she had. I think she knew that her time was up."

Neither of them said anything for a few minutes. Iris guessed that Mike was having the same thoughts as her. A visit from the spirit of Harold was the sign of a death to come.

"All of these revelations, apart from giving the curse a lot of credence, also made me think about choices I've made. Although I didn't know all the details of the deaths, I knew about Becky and I knew there were other children who had died."

Mike got up from the table and grabbed a bottle of wine. When he had poured glasses for them both, he continued.

"When we met…When we met, I knew you were the one for me. I also knew that there was some risk attached for anyone that married me. Originally, I thought that meant that any children we had might meet an early end. That's why I told you that I didn't want any."

A sob escaped and Mike took a second to compose himself.

"It seemed a good solution at the time. Then, after a while, I began to worry about that decision. Was I denying you something that you really wanted? Would you leave me for someone who wanted a family? I started to withdraw. I didn't know how to talk to you about it. If I had sprung this on you, the story of the curse, you would have definitely run a mile."

Iris took a large gulp of wine. Tears were in her eyes, as well.

"I followed you to your night school class a couple of times. I thought that you were probably having an affair. Not that I would have blamed you. I wasn't communicating, I just sat in my chair watching television, day in and day out. Then when you came home and said that you'd been saved from a mugging by a ghost. Well, that made me think about mum's stories. Obviously, I ignored it and hoped it would all go away."

A small grin from Mike before he carried on.

"Then there were more incidents and I had to look into the stuff that mum had left. As grim as it all is, we needed to know."

Iris was looking at the ring that had been in the box. Her fierce concentration was helping her to hold back from crying.

"The ring. There was a story about that too. Mum thought that it might be cursed, so she threw it away. Next day it was back again. On the kitchen table. She tried again, throwing it into a bin in the town centre, but, yes, it came back again."

"That's a bit of a terrifying story to leave until last, Mike."

A loud, harsh voice came out of her, surprising them both.

"Sorry, but that's pretty significant. Even if you write all the deaths off as bizarre accidents, a ring that you can't get rid of is a solid clue that something spooky is going on."

"I know. I got caught up in all the facts and figures. Typical of me, I suppose. I just have that sort of mind where I want everything in order. How do you put up with me?"

"I don't put up with you, Mike, I love you."

"Even with the curse?"

"Yes."

Chapter 15

Iris was reeling after all the information she had been hit with. Mike hadn't even told her about some of the deaths. What she had learned, so far, was quite enough for the moment. Setting aside the stories of the family curse, she had also just discovered that her husband had a sister called Becky, who had died at the age of 6.

Why would he not tell her about such an important part of his life? At first, she had been horrified by the manner of the death and then she had felt resentful, because he had not bothered to even mention Becky. A bit of reflection made her realise that it was a lot more complicated than that.

Iris understood that if Mike had told her about Becky, he would have had to tell her about the curse. The fact that he was adamant that he didn't want children was tied into it, as well. Without Harold appearing to her, she would never have believed what he was saying. A ghost, a curse and accidents which were, somehow, manufactured.

Mike was a man of numbers. He was very keen on facts. Solid, reliable facts. Ask him something and he probably knew the answer. Her own encyclopaedia. To hear this tale from him, without her experiences, would have been bizarre. Her whole world had shifted on its axis and she needed her husband more than ever now.

It would be tough for him, but Iris knew that she must get him to talk about his family. Like a lot of men, he had taken his feelings and emotions and locked them away. No word of Becky, his parents' deaths just described as a car accident and, lately, his difficulties talking to her. Time to help him deal with all the baggage.

"You've never talked much about your parents and I didn't even know about Becky. I'd like to know more about them." Iris said.

"My dad, Terry, was a quiet man. I'm similar to him in appearance. He was tall and dark, but a bit stooped, even as a young man. I think it was a physical reaction to his childhood. His brother Phillip died when he was fifteen. He was the one that was killed by the logs falling off of the lorry. I don't think he ever got over it. Add to that, what happened to Becky, and he was full of sadness.

"He tried, though, for my sake. He loved football and would take me to matches. I don't remember him ever taking a day off work sick. He got up each day and, through sheer determination, got things done. He would smile and joke with me, but I could sense the struggle that he always had.

"My mum, Penny, was the small bubbly type. She made my dad smile and I recall my younger years being happy because of her. Mum taking me and Becky swimming. Taking us to the cinema. Holidays on the coast. Everything changed with Becky's death.

"My sister. I didn't tell you about her, not because she was forgotten. It was like I'd filed her away. A painful memory that I didn't want to bring up. I had to talk about the deaths of my parents and I didn't want to make my life sound even more tragic than it already was. I wanted to think about Becky laughing and playing, not being taken away in an ambulance.

"It's nearly thirty years since she died and I don't have many memories of her. There are pictures of her that I look at occasionally, just to remind myself what she looked like. I don't want to forget her, but I don't want to remember, if that makes sense. You didn't know about her, so anniversaries of her death and her birthday would pass without any fuss.

"Once she was gone, my mum changed. As a result of that, my dad changed and I did, too, I suppose, but to a lesser extent. We lost the light in our family and my dad was quieter than before. Mum was, of course, absorbed by the whole curse thing. I became independent. Mum was preoccupied, dad was distant, so I had to get on with stuff without their input.

"I'm making it sound awful, but it just became the norm. I still felt loved and cared for. It was done in a different way, though. I went through school, then university, made friends and even snagged myself a gorgeous wife. Things lurk in the background, but it didn't affect me. Not until I thought about the, having children, thing and then I tied myself in knots."

"We've faced that one, now. We've had this talk. I think we understand each other a bit more as a result. I wish I had known about Becky, but I understand why you didn't want to talk about her. When your parents died. That must have been awful."

"It was. Especially after mum and I had talked about the curse a few weeks before. I was your typical bloke of twenty-one. Not interested in anything emotional or drama filled. I can remember squirming as mum told me about ghosts and deaths. I couldn't wait for the conversation to be over. I didn't want to think about it and then when they died…it was too much.

"She had given me the box and said that all her research was in it. She hoped that I would never have to open it. I shoved it in the loft and tried to forget about it. The bizarre manner of the accident tied in with a lot of, what I thought were, her crazy ideas, and I couldn't face it. Now I know a lot more than I ever wanted to."

"I never asked to see pictures of your family. I guessed that it was difficult for you, but I'd like to, now. I'm looking at photos of your ancestors, but I haven't seen them."

"I'll get them."

Chapter 16

As Mike talked he had faced a number of things. The biggest emotion was guilt. He hadn't thought about his sister enough. He hadn't thought about his parents enough. He hadn't told Iris about them. No wonder he found it so hard to communicate, when he couldn't even tell her about his family.

What he had gleaned from his mother's notes, was that a ghost, Harold, appeared to a member of the Thomas family and befriended them. This was a prelude to them dying in a bizarre accident. Stories of smoke or mist at the site of the deaths, guardian angels and imaginary friends, all indicated that this was the modus operandi.

Mike had wasted so much time, in self-doubt and denial, and now Iris was being threatened. A typical bloke, he had avoided all confrontation and discussion of feelings. It was now pouring out in one massive gush and it was hugely uncomfortable for him. Thinking about something happening to his wife, left him barely able to hold it all together.

On a roll now, he ploughed on. Get it all out there.

"I'm sorry I never told you about Becky and my parents. I'm sorry that I've not been able to talk to you about important things. I could see it all slipping away, but I couldn't find the words to stop it."

"It works both ways, Mike. I knew that something was wrong, but I didn't confront it either. How stupid are we? Two grown people who love each other and can't talk about basic things. Look at me. I'm adopted and have a whole family out there somewhere that I know nothing about. Don't want to know about them. Can't be bothered to find out about them, because my parents are so great. Scared to find out about them and, maybe, be rejected. I don't know which it is."

"I've dumped a load of stuff on you today. Not just the curse, but the children thing, too. You've not had a lot of time to process it all. Any thoughts?"

"You told me from the beginning that you didn't want children. I married you knowing that. I understand why you feel that way now. This whole Harold thing is having a huge impact on our lives and I don't like it. He is dictating, from beyond the grave, whether we have a family and who lives and dies. I'm terrified and I'm angry and I need to consider all of this for a while."

"We don't know anything for sure yet. This could all be coincidence. If you think about it, a ghost killing people seems far-fetched. The main thing, at the moment, is that we are talking. Really talking. I hated the silence between us, even though it was my fault. I don't ever want that to happen again." Mike said.

"We make an agreement, here and now, to keep talking. It looks like we are going to have some tough topics to cover, but we must face them. We've got to get back to the way we were. We used to go out and have fun. Meals and holidays. Shopping together. At the moment, if we both want to watch the same television programme, that is the highlight of our week. We've not been living. We just make it through one day after another."

"Agreed. The new regime starts now. Let's top up our wine and drink to that. We are going to be hungover in the morning anyway, we might as well finish the bottle."

Mike had made a positive speech. We don't know anything, far-fetched, coincidence. On the other hand, there was lots of, albeit circumstantial, evidence that Harold was at large and creating these accidents. The notes his mother had made, kept whirring in his head. Had the death certificates and newspaper clippings not been there, he would have doubted the events happened.

Always fastidious, he was in charge of finances, Mike wanted to verify what he had seen. Some of what his mother had recorded was hearsay and family lore. The talk of ghosts, particularly. Iris, however, had now had her own encounters and that made it more real. He could cling to the hope that it was all some crazy legend and nothing bad would happen, but there was enough doubt to make him very worried.

Chapter 17

Iris and Mike talked into the night about his family and their relationship. Apologies, explanations and promises for the future. How much of a future there would be was a topic to be covered another time. Information needed to be absorbed and considered before they discussed it further.

It was late when they went to bed. Despite being weary, sleep eluded them. Iris couldn't quite believe that this was happening to her. The, seemingly, benign visits from Harold meant that she was marked to die in some weird, possibly comical, way. At the moment there was no fear, only resignation. That, of course, might change.

The curse was a real thing. It was all nonsense. Iris vacillated between these two standpoints for most of the night. Interspersed with that worry, were thoughts about what Mike had said. He didn't want children because of the curse. It was not surprising that the next morning, she felt and looked dreadful.

An extra layer of makeup helped a bit, but Iris was not keen to leave the house. Part of her reluctance was due to her fatigue and part was due to the fear of dying. Hovering at the front door, she gave herself a good talking to and stepped outside. Approaching the car, she hesitated again. There were dozens of ways to die in that thing.

Her knuckles were white around the car keys. A moment to gain courage and then she was inside. The engine started and she checked her seatbelt a few times before exiting the drive onto their quiet road. That was bad enough. Hitting the main roads would be terrifying. Each junction was a minefield and every pedestrian was a distraction. It took an extra ten minutes to complete her fifteen minutes journey.

"You're a bit late. Oh, Iris, you look terrible."

"Thanks."

Iris tried to smile at Wendy, but it was more of a grimace.

"Are you alright?"

"Just had a bad night."

"You need to talk about anything?"

Her hackles went down and Iris gave Wendy a hug.

"Thanks, Wendy. I'm okay. I appreciate your offer, though."

"Well, I'll make a cuppa. The cure for everything, that."

Iris imagined taking a gulp and the tea bag still being in the cup and then lodging in her throat. That would be a good one, wouldn't it, Harold. She would check to make sure that couldn't happen.

An examination of her workplace didn't reveal any obvious dangers. No bare wires or trip hazards. No way for a homicidal customer to get through the glass at the counter. Of course, a plane could crash into the building. No way to guard herself from that. Time to open the doors to the public. That would be a distraction from thinking about how she was going to die.

The usual suspects filed through the door. The job involved forms and money and looking after people. The job needed concentration. At lunchtime she took tiny bites of her sandwich, choking had become a preoccupation, and then the slow torturous journey home in the death car.

Iris practically fell into the house, so eager was she for its sanctuary. Viewing the cooker with suspicion, and glad that it was electric not gas, she started preparing the evening meal. Rubber soled shoes, to protect against electrocution. Leather gloves in case the knife slipped. Such was her focus, that Mike had been watching her for a couple of minutes before she noticed him.

"Taking a few precautions?"

"Bearing in mind what may be in my future, I thought it wise. No point in making it easy for Harold."

"I'm going to get changed, then we'll have dinner and then I think we need to talk."

Dinner, tiny bites again, took a while and then they settled in the lounge with cups of tea and stared at each other. Iris broke the ice.

"Today was horrible. I was scared in the car, at work, cooking, afraid of everything. Harold has visited me, in the same way he has done previously with other victims, and it is an indication that my cards are marked. I know he's coming for me. I can drive slowly, check my surroundings and wear gloves, but he can strike at any time, in any place. I can't relax for a second and that makes life impossible."

"I know, I know. I've been thinking about it all day. Worrying about you."

"The dozens of, are you alright, messages indicated that."

"What can we do?"

"All those Thomas's who died in the past. They didn't know they were marked for death. The ghost that appeared wasn't seen as a harbinger of doom. They did nothing to protect themselves."

"My mum knew what was going on. She couldn't escape her fate."

"Did she try? I mean, did she just accept what was going to happen, or did she look into a way to stop it?"

"I think she just let it happen. That sounds bad, but I'm sure she thought that there was nothing she could do. How do you fight a ghost?"

"That is a very interesting question. I'm going to get my laptop and see if I can find anything."

"What are you going to search for? How to get rid of a ghost. Protection from an evil spirit. You will find a whole load of crackpots, eager to take our money, but unable to really help."

"Quite frankly, Mike, I'm willing to try anything if it will keep me alive."

"Yes, of course. I don't want us to go chasing shadows. We need to think this through and make a plan."

Iris couldn't help smiling. Even in the face of the impossible, a murderous ghostly ancestor, Mike wanted to make a plan.

"I understand. Let me have a look and see if there is anything and then we'll go from there."

Chapter 18

"Good Lord, Mike, there are lots of sites dedicated to ghost management."

"Ghost management?"

"That's what some of them call it. It's all a bit bewildering."

"Does any of it look legit? I can't believe I'm asking that. Let's stop for a minute. Ghosts, spirits, swirls of mist, we don't even know what we are dealing with."

"I'm going with ghost, but that is a whole new discussion. We're talking God and heaven and hell. Why do some people linger and not move on? How do they do it? What is the space between life and death?"

"Some thorny subjects in that list. I suppose that it all stems from what you believe. Do you think that one's spirit, or soul, goes somewhere after death?"

"I don't know. Should it just disappear? If so, what keeps it here?"

"Strong emotions might be the tie. Harold was full of hate and that's what keeps him hanging around."

"In films and things, you have to find the cause of the spirits unrest and then help them pass over."

"That is fiction, Iris."

"But it must be based on something. Why have stories like that been around for millennia?"

"There are stories about werewolves and vampires and space aliens, too. All of these things have an element of truth, which has warped and been embellished over the years."

"An element of truth. I think we have to start with that. I'm going to do some research. Old manuscripts and things like that. I'll also look for reports from people who have been haunted. Maybe we can find someone who has dealt with a spirit successfully."

Mike got his computer, too, and they both dug deep into the world of ghosts and ghouls. Supposedly, true life stories, legends, lots of fiction and some, dubious advice were found. It was difficult navigating through the rubbish to find anything that might be of value. Mike was getting exasperated.

"If I read one more thing about sage smudging, I think I'm going to scream. None of this is helpful. We need to find something that will actually make a difference. Have you had any luck?"

"Only the scary stuff seems to be of any use. Seances and exorcisms."

"Exorcisms, isn't that to get rid of a demon that is possessing someone?"

"It can also get rid of a spirit from a place."

"The problem with that, Iris, is that Harold doesn't seem to stay in one place."

"I know, but I'm getting desperate. What do you think about a séance?"

"I can't help but picture one of those aging women in a fringed shawl, rolling her eyes and speaking in a phony voice."

"I know exactly what you mean. That puts me off, as well as contacting spirits and stirring up trouble. In the films it always makes things worse."

"How could it make things worse? Okay. Have you found anyone that does seances and doesn't sound like a charlatan?"

"Oof, how do you tell who is okay? I've looked at dozens of adverts and articles and I can't work it out. I suppose that we have to talk to some of them, see if we can get a feel for whether they can help."

"We'd better crack on with this. Time is not on our side. Iris, could you take a few days off work? I worry about you driving and being more susceptible outside of the house."

"Mike. Harold is going to find a way to kill me, whether I'm at home or not."

"We don't have to make it easy for him. Take a few days off and then that will give you time to find a medium and also do more research. Ring in sick in the morning. You're never off, so they can't complain. Please. Put yourself first and focus on finding a way to deal with this curse."

"Okay."

Iris nodded and went to Mike and hugged him.

"Back to research then."

The rest of the evening was spent tapping on keyboards, making notes and passing an occasional comment. Iris had five names on her list of prospective mediums. Middle aged women seemed to be the main demographic for that role. The moment she saw a Paisley pattern or a tassel they would be scratched off.

The hardest thing to do was to lie to her work colleagues. Thinking back, Wendy had asked her what was wrong, so she might get away with it. What reason would she give, though? I'm hiding from a murderous spirit, might be the truth, but it wasn't the type of thing to share. A bad headache would only do for one day. A nasty cold it was then.

Iris did the rasping voice on the phone and Wendy was full of sympathy.

"I'll tell the boss and he will have to come and man the front line with me. It'll be hell, but I forgive you. Feel better soon, Iris. You're never off, so if you need a few days, make sure you take them."

Staring at her phone and then the list, Iris wondered what the hell she was doing. Then she thought about Harold and knew that an extraordinary problem needed an extraordinary remedy. Here we go, she thought.

Chapter 19

Mike found himself daydreaming at work. A conscientious employee, he jolted back to the job and focussed on the computer in front of him. Within seconds he was drifting away again. The last few days had brought back a lot of memories. Now all he could think about was Becky.

Small, dark haired, a beaming, gap toothed smile. It was a vivid picture. Seeing the photographs had reminded him of their childhood. Becky in a goal, marked by two flowerpots, grimacing as he ran up to kick the ball. He would either score a goal or fire it straight at her. A scream and a dive out of the way. She would save maybe one out of ten of his shots and that was enough to keep her happy.

They argued, of course. A favourite pencil, whose turn it was to chose a film to watch. Not another cartoon princess. Then there was running and laughing. Building a fort. Doing a jigsaw puzzle. His eyes misted at the thought of the good times. The image of the ambulance outside of the house and his confusion, eventually, pushed the happiness away.

That brought him to his mother. There had, surely, never been a more horrific sight than his mother buckling at the knees and being caught by his father. Her garbled words, the only one that either he or his father could make out was "Becky". The sense that something had gone terribly wrong. Something about Becky.

It had taken him a while to understand what had happened. Even when he had heard the words "Becky's dead" he hadn't taken it in. The funeral and all the crying had been the proof he needed and had allowed him to start to grieve for his sister. Dealing with his own sorrow was derailed by the unsettling changes to his mother.

It was during the few months after his sister's death that his mother was most disturbed. Understandable, but it was more than just grief. She had a manic need to find an explanation for Becky's death. Yes, she had been stung by a swarm of bees. A random event. Not as far as she was concerned.

Mike's father had worked hard to supply the stable environment that his sone needed. There was some latitude, but he put his foot down, after four months, and told his wife to focus on the child that they still had. Things got better, but were never the same. An obsession had been born in the time since Becky died. An investigation into the curse.

There had been some awareness of his mother's preoccupation. Paperwork and pieces of paper. Correspondence going back and forth. Death certificates, newspaper clippings and scrawled notes were strewn across every surface. When he was younger, they were swept out of the way in case he saw upsetting details. Later they were left in place.

University was a welcome escape. When he was home during the holidays, his mother did her best to focus on him and not her research. Then came the conversation. The frantic relaying of information which scared him more than he had ever admitted. He knew some of it by osmosis. He had been in the house where the notes and the talk were.

"Mike. I need to talk to you. Put the paper down. You need to pay attention to what I'm going to say. You know I've been looking into the Thomas family curse. If you can stop rolling your eyes and sighing this will go a lot more smoothly."

Her face was drawn. Mike noticed how many lines there were on her forehead and around her mouth. Years of worry had taken their toll.

"Okay, the curse. I've looked into your dad's family history and I'm convinced that there is a curse. There have been so many bizarre deaths of young members of the family over the last few generations. There has been talk of a ghost appearing and it being an indication that tragedy is about to strike. I'm worried that…"

Mike watched as his mother struggled for the next words. He knew now what she had been on the verge of saying. She had seen the ghost.

"Anyway. This box is full of my research. There are photographs and notes, certificates and articles from newspapers. Everything I've discovered is in there. This is why Becky died. Becky and so many other children in the Thomas family. Should you have children of your own, one day, something similar may happen to you. All the information you need is in this box."

She hadn't said that this conversation was in case she died, but they both knew what the unsaid part was. Not ready to even contemplate his mother's death, Mike had simply nodded and looked at the box.

It wasn't the last chat that they ever had, but it was the most memorable. Then the news of his parent's death had come to him and he had been shocked, but not at all surprised. The nature of the accident had unnerved him. The box was left to gather dust. Mike didn't want to know what it contained.

The noise of his office door opening recalled him to the present. Calculations and data needed his attention. Iris. He had to find a way to protect her.

Chapter 20

Candidate number one, on the list of mediums, was scratched off the list after a few seconds. Brief introductions were followed by a mention of the cost. Iris didn't get a chance to discuss what she needed and why. There was no opportunity to question the person about her skill and experience. Who knew what the price for a séance was, but this first quote seemed expensive.

The next call was to a lady named Judy. A soft voice said hello and that was already a much better start than the previous call.

"Oh, hello. My name's Iris and I need someone to hold a séance for me."

"Okay, Iris. I'm going to ask you a few questions to see what you need. Is that alright?"

"Yes, sounds good."

"First of all, are you trying to contact someone specific?"

"Yes."

"A member of your family?"

"My husband's."

"Will he be there, too? Your husband, I mean."

"Yes."

"Is there a particular thing that you want to ask?"

"I think it's best if I set out the scenario for you. It's not straightforward. We are having problems with a disgruntled spirit. Research into Mike's, my husband's, ancestors have revealed a series of bizarre deaths, referred to as "The Curse", now thought to have been caused by the intervention of Harold Thomas, who died in 1918."

The first of a series of gasps and expletives was uttered by Judy at that statement. As the story unfolded and examples of the strange deaths were given, the "oh dears" and "good Lords" were replaced with a couple of "bloody hells".

"So, you've actually seen a manifestation of Harold."

"Yes. My friend Mel was with me the last time. She saw the mist swirl away after it had shoved the bloke with the beer, as well"

"Amazing. And terrifying of course. I've seen things, but others usually can't. The fact that he shows himself to you is odd. All part of his method I suppose. Make you think he is friendly and then he pounces."

"That seems to be it."

"Time is of the essence. A threat is hanging over you and we need to know how to stop it. I think, if I can see your research, it would be helpful for when we do the séance. How soon can I come around and see you?"

Iris arranged for Judy to come for a visit the following evening. She would be able to brief Mike on their conversation and he could get his papers in order. She looked at the other names on the list of mediums and wondered if she should call them. Judy had been warm, reassuring and she had, the most important point, believed the story without hesitation. She had found the person she was looking for.

Judy had a website and Iris had a look at it. The page was relatively plain. No candles or Ouija boards. No runes or ectoplasm. Judy described the discovery of her gift as a child.

…My mother asked who I was talking to and I said it was grandma. She had passed the year before. "Ah, you have the gift.", she said. Thank goodness she was so understanding of what was happening. She helped me to hone my skills. As a teenager I began to think it was a curse, but as I grew older, I realised that I could help people…

A few testimonials were featured on the site and some suggestions for what might be a suitable contribution for her services. Understated and professional, Iris thought. Her decision was looking even better.

The conversation with Judy had reminded her that she had not been in touch with Mel. Her friend had experienced

Harold's presence, too. It was a lot to deal with and Mel had been left to do that on her own. Time for a chat. Iris had decided not to tell her about the curse, but within a minute, the conversation took a turn.

"What do you mean you have been marked for death?" Mel wailed.

"The ghost appears to someone and then tries to kill them."

"Am I going to die, too?"

"No, only members of the Thomas family. Look, it's complicated."

"I'm coming around after work. You have to tell me all about it. I've got to go now. The boss is giving me the evil eye."

The immediate reaction to that statement was that Iris put a couple of bottles of wine in the fridge. Mel would want all the details and would need something to bolster her as she learned about evil great, great, however many times, uncle Harold.

Mike came through the front door, he was home early, to be given two lots of startling news.

"I've arranged for a medium to come here tomorrow evening. She wants to see your research to help her prepare for the séance. Oh, and Mel will be here soon."

"Hang on a minute. You found a medium?"

"Yes. Her name is Judy. She seems very nice."

"You phoned everyone on the list then."

"No. Only two. She was the second. Don't tell me off or lecture me. I didn't need to call anyone else. I got a good feeling speaking to her. When you meet her tomorrow, you will understand."

"Did you tell Mel? Is that why she's coming over?"

"Yes, a bit of it. I need to tell her everything."

"Is there wine in the fridge? Okay, I'll get the takeaway menus."

Chapter 21

Judy had a day time job. She cooked at a local café, the morning shift. A blur of eggs and bacon, beans and toast. She could do it with her eyes closed. The work wasn't thrilling, but the banter with the customers, many of them regular, was what kept her going. Her role as a medium was totally separate to her job in the kitchen.

The usual requests that she got were from friends and family of the recently deceased. They wanted to be reassured that their relative was happy in the afterlife. Some wanted to ask questions and some wanted to pass on their final message. They wanted forgiveness. They wanted explanations. They wanted, quite often, to know where the money was.

There was no specific fee for her services, but people were, usually, generous. If she was the bearer of bad news, they were less likely to hand over the money. Sometimes, she couldn't contact the person that they wanted to speak to. Why this happened, she didn't know. The one thing she wouldn't do, was fake it. This was serious business for her.

There were people out there working the con. They had a talent of a sort, but it wasn't the one that she had. The, alleged, mediums could go into a house, scan the photographs and keepsakes in a room and make educated guesses about the deceased. Careful questioning and being aware of tone and body language and they could twist and turn into a believable narrative.

This call from Iris was something out of the ordinary. A malevolent ghost that attacked and killed people as part of a vendetta. A spirit that had lingered long after his death and caused mayhem and sorrow. This Harold had to be dealt with. How she would deal with him, was a whole new problem.

"Alright, Mum. Internet, phone, notes, what are you doing?"

Daniel, her son had arrived home from work and was peering over her shoulder.

"I've been asked to do a séance and it is different from anything I've done before. I'm trying to get some ideas on how to handle it."

"What's different about this one?"

"It's dealing with a disgruntled spirit."

"You take care. I know they can throw stuff around."

"Don't worry."

She didn't discuss her medium work with him. It wasn't that he didn't believe in it, it was more that he stood back out of the way and let her do what she needed to do. There was no way that she would share with Daniel that this ghost was suspected of murder. He would not be happy with her getting involved. The fact that he was a policeman, complicated matters, as well.

The only thing to do was call up Harold and see what she would be facing. If she could persuade him to move on, the job would be done. A person who lingered after death and then started killing members of his family, was not likely to go quietly.

At the moment, it was all supposition. Once Judy had seen the evidence that Iris's husband had gathered, it would become clearer. Part of her doubted what she had been told, but Iris had been level headed and sounded frightened. It felt important to try to help them, so that's what she would do.

Chapter 22

Mike and Mel got on well. It had been added confirmation, for Iris, that he was the right one for her. Her friend wouldn't have allowed her to marry someone who was not suitable. A desperate, clingy, group hug happened when Mel came through the door. Sat at the kitchen table, Mike related the story of the curse.

It was an abridged version. A bit of background about Harold and the circumstances that had made him so bitter. After that it was a list of people dying. Various profanities escaped from Mel's lips as she listened to the strange and gruesome ways that members of the Thomas family died.

The part where the ghostly appearances were mentioned had Mel yelling.

"YES, yes. I saw it myself."

Mike finished the story by telling of the loss of his parents and his sister.

"I didn't know you had a sister." Mel wailed.

"Neither did I." Iris whispered.

"Oh, Iris."

"Mike didn't want to tell me and I understand. It was all part of a story he hoped I would never learn about."

"Good God, you two have had to deal with a lot. I'm still trying to take it all in. The conclusion, it appears, is that Iris will be killed soon, by Harold, in some terrible way."

"That's about it, Mel." Mike confirmed.

The next ten minutes were spent consoling a weeping Mel. A box of tissues and a top up of wine helped to bring her back from the edge.

"I've got so many things I want to ask. Mike, have you known about this curse for a long time?"

"Yes and no. I got a short, garbled version from my mum, who'd been a bit bonkers since Becky died, so I decided to ignore it. The appearance of the ghost made me look in the box of papers she had insisted I keep."

"Why do you think Harold has picked on Iris? He's mainly gone for children."

"That is a very good question." Iris looked at Mike waiting for an answer.

"I knew, from my mum's brief tale, that children in the Thomas family were cursed. I told Iris, from the beginning, that I didn't want kids. I thought it would save us from the heartache of losing a son or a daughter. Maybe, Harold, having been thwarted from taking our child, is going after Iris instead."

"Can you do anything to stop it?"

"That, Mel, is the thing we have been working on. At the moment, the only thing we have come up with, is to have a séance and see if we can talk to Harold and reason with him in some way. I've arranged for a woman named Judy to come around tomorrow."

"I think I ought to be here. For the séance, I mean. I have seen the ghost, or the mist, after all."

"What do you think, Mike? Can Mel come to the séance?"

"Why not. I'll need to get more wine, though."

Two empty bottles stood on the table and Mike was getting a third. He would have a hangover at work the next morning, but if ever there was an excuse for over indulging, this was it.

"So…"

Mel started to talk, but had a bout of hiccups. Once under control she carried on.

"So, what way do you think he might kill you, Iris?"

"Let's see. What has Harold done so far. Bees, sucked out of a train, falling masonry, stampeding horse, um…"

"Tripped, on a cat, through a plate glass window."

"Oh yes, thank you Mike. Cow in the road, poison mushrooms, probably some more that I can't think of now. Anyway, a wide variety of ways. Harold doesn't like to repeat himself."

"He's kept up to date, too. Horse, then train and then a car." Mike pointed out.

"Okay. What's really modern that could kill you?" Mel frowned with concentration. "A mobile phone."

"How would that kill someone, Mel?" Mike asked.

"Um… not sure."

"Maybe, I'm concentrating on my phone and I walk off of a cliff."

Iris giggled. Mel giggled. There was no getting any sense out of them after that. Mike went to the lounge and put the television on. Every now and then he heard hysterical laughter from the kitchen. When the laughter turned to tears, he returned to restore order.

"You girls alright?"

"A bit drunk and a bit sad." Iris informed him.

"I better get home. I need to sober up and then I've got work in the morning. Then we get to do it all again with Judy."

"I'll call you a taxi."

"Thanks, Mike. I love you and Iris. You are such great friends. I can't bear the thought of…"

More crying and hugging and then the taxi came and Mel had to act a bit more normal when she left the house. Mike and Iris sat at the kitchen table, surrounded by glasses, bottles and plates.

"We best get to bed, too. I've got work tomorrow and then we've got Judy coming."

"You're right."

Something happened that night, which hadn't happened for a while. Mike and Iris made love. There was more than a bit of desperation about it. Intense is what Iris thought. They were finding each other again when the end of their relationship was nigh.

Chapter 23

Iris spent the day cleaning the house. A good distraction from the oppressive thoughts of death. The worry didn't go completely, but being at home felt safer than being outside.

Mel sent a message saying that her head hurt, not surprising, but that she would be back that night to see what Judy had to say. Many thanks were sent back. A boozy night with her friend was just what she had needed.

Mike's piles of notes were on the kitchen table and Iris found herself reading them again. The details had been scary enough when spoken, seeing them written down provoked a new level of despair. The spoken words had floated away and she could almost pretend that they had never been said. On paper they were tangible.

Soup for lunch, much safer than solids and then a good hour trying on outfits. What did one wear for a séance? T shirt and jeans was the final choice. Very plain, the opposite of all the frills and prints of the archetypal medium. Hopefully, Judy would be similarly attired. Iris was putting a lot of faith in her and she wanted Mike to trust her, too. If she turned up in the whole fortune teller outfit, he would be immediately turned off.

Mike came home from work with a couple of carrier bags of food and wine.

"I thought we should have snacks. I wasn't sure what sort of things to serve at a séance, so I've kept it simple. Peanuts, crisps, a couple of dips. Not practical if we have to hold hands, I suppose, but maybe for before, or after."

Iris hugged him. What a bizarre set of circumstances they had found themselves in.

"I think peanuts, crisps and dips are just perfect. You got wine, too, I hope."

"Gallons of the stuff. We should have enough, as long as Judy doesn't knock it back like you and Mel."

The snacks were distributed into dishes and they grabbed a sandwich before anyone arrived. The doorbell rang and the first visitor was Mel. They had barely poured the wine, when Judy turned up.

"Come in, Judy. It's nice to meet you in person. This is my husband, Mike and this is my friend Mel. She was there when Harold appeared the last time."

"I'm very pleased to meet you all."

The medium looked nothing like Iris had imagined. There had been no photo on the website, so she had been free to picture Judy how she liked. In her mind, a woman of around fifty, smart, but a bit drab, with brown hair. In reality, a tiny blonde, in jeans and a pink jacket. The handbag she was carrying seemed enormous next to her petite frame. She was all business, though.

"Right. Iris gave me the basics, but, Mike, if you could give me more details that will help."

Mike and Judy sat at the table while Iris and Mel lurked in the background clasping wine glasses. Judy had turned down the offer of a drink. She wanted to stay focused on the job in hand.

As the tale of the curse unfolded, Mel and Iris still shuddered as each of the deaths was disclosed. Judy jotted things down in a pink notebook. She asked a few questions in her calm, soft voice and nodded and wrote.

"Okay. Thank you, Mike. This is a fascinating and frightening story. It certainly seems that Harold has decided to stay after death and take his revenge on the Thomas family. Often spirits will manifest in some way. Things move around a house. Doors and windows open and close. I've never seen anything as malevolent as this. You are fearful for Iris's wellbeing and want to make contact to see if you can stop anything from happening."

"That's about it." Mike nodded and then looked to Iris and Mel, who nodded in confirmation.

"Take a moment to think about what you want to say to Harold if he appears. I suggest that we aim for a conciliatory tone. I don't think anger and recriminations, however justified, will help dissuade him from his course of action."

"I better keep quiet then, because I'm mad as hell." Mel said.

"Do you know, Judy, where dead people usually go? I'm thinking that we could ask him to move on. Say that, surely, he has avenged the deaths of his wife and son many times over. It is now time to leave and find peace."

"I'll be honest with you Iris, I'm not sure. The spirits that I talk to are often hanging around in a kind of halfway house. They want to pass on a message or right a wrong. Very few want some kind of retribution. No one really says where they have been or where they are going. Believe me, many clients ask those questions. Some of the deceased can't, or won't, respond when I try to reach them. Have they passed onto another place? Are they just gone?"

"My thoughts are, that if he has spent decades killing people, he's not likely to pass peacefully onto heaven. It might be tough asking him to stop what he's doing and go to hell."

"Indeed, Mike."

"The only thing I can think of, is to say that he has got his revenge. He's ruined many lives and that must have sated his desire to inflict pain on the Thomas family. It's time to stop."

Mike held Iris's hand.

"We'll try that."

"How do we do this then?" Mel asked.

Iris looked at each of the people in the room and a shiver ran through her. They were really going to do it. What if they made things worse? What if Harold attacked them in some way? Perhaps he wouldn't turn up at all and they would all feel a little foolish. It was too late to back out now. Reminding herself that she was under a death sentence, Iris moved towards the table and sat down. Mel did the same and they looked at Judy and waited.

Chapter 24

Judy outlined the next steps.

"There are no strict rules on how to hold a séance. I did some research, when I first started, and there was a lot of conflicting advice. I have my own routine that works for me. We won't be turning the lights off and sitting in the dark with a candle. That's just theatrics. We will be holding hands, though. There is a common purpose here and that helps to focus our energies."

"I'm a bit worried, about a lot of things really, but mainly about Harold turning up and hurting someone." Iris fidgeted as she spoke.

"If things get scary, I will break contact and bring the séance to an end. I know that Harold can turn up at various places without being called, but in this case, having asked him to attend, I can ask him to stop."

"There's no time like the present. Let's get started." Mike held out his hands and they all linked up.

"I am going to be quiet for a while. I need to concentrate on Harold. As soon as we make contact, I will let you know."

Judy closed her eyes and sat very still. Iris glanced at the others and then they all lowered their heads and were lost in their own thoughts. She was tempted to giggle, just to relieve the tension and because she was terrified. Then the air seemed to change. The goose pimples rose across her arms and Mel let out a tiny whimper. Mike squeezed her hand and they waited.

"Harold, are you with us?" Judy opened her eyes as she spoke.

There was a hiss, rather than a word, but they all knew it was him. No mist swirling or items moving, just a chill in the air and a sense of dread.

"You know why you are here. The curse that you have put upon the Thomas family, has caused suffering for generations. We know that you suffered, too, when you lost your wife and son, but this vendetta has to end." Judy took a measured tone.

The reply was the word, no, followed by a cackling laugh.

"Please don't take Iris from me. I love her, like you loved Edith. You took my sister, Becky and my parents. We have paid your price." Mike begged.

A mist formed and swirled around the table, causing them all to shrink away from it. It moved faster and faster and then swooped towards Iris and settled on her for a second. The wail that emanated from the spirit brought Mike to his feet, ready to defend his wife from whatever happened next.

A couple of plates shattered on the floor as everything in the room shook. Everyone clung to the table and Mel let out a scream.

"STOP IT." Iris's cry brought a response.

Thwarted for now, but I will be back.

Harold spoke and then the mist disappeared.

Judy clapped her hands, to make sure he was gone, and they all slumped back in their chairs.

"What the hell did that mean?" Mel said what they were all thinking.

Baffled looks were exchanged and then the discussion began.

"First of all, bloody hell. We've just been talking to a ghost. The mist and the voice. I would never have believed it if I hadn't seen it with my own eyes. That was amazing and horrible all at the same time." Mel was still wide eyed and shaking.

"That was terrifying. I don't know, Judy, do you get some vibe or anything from spirits? If so, what do you think of Harold?" Iris asked.

"Nothing good, I'm afraid. I could feel his hate. In fact, all I could feel was hate. That last statement. I don't know what it means. Do any of you have an idea?"

"Not a clue." Mike said and no one else offered an explanation.

"That mist thing. Was that just to intimidate Iris? The wail afterwards was awful." Mel shuddered at the memory.

"We wanted to find out about him. Maybe he wanted to find out more about us. Iris in particular. That type of manifestation is quite rare. I didn't see Harold, the man, at any time, only his feelings. The mist was the only representation of him."

"We did find out more about him. He's pure evil. It's a case of know your enemy, I suppose. We tried to appeal to him, but he is heartless and determined. That means we have to find another way of dealing with him."

"That final bit. "Thwarted for now, but I will be back". What's, "for now"? Does that mean that we have more time to work this out?" Iris was trying to find a positive.

"I've been wracking my brains and I can't think what it means. We need to keep working at this. Act as if time is still of the essence. Let's sleep on it and then see if we can come up with a new strategy. Judy, we are grateful for your help. I was still hoping that this was not real, but after tonight, there is no denying that Harold is haunting us and planning something bad." Mike said.

"Thank you, Judy. You brought him here and we made our plea, but it doesn't seem to have made any difference. Harold still seems intent on coming after me."

"I'm with you now. I'll be thinking about this and trying to come up with an idea, too. If you think of something, give me a ring and we can call Harold back again."

"That's very kind Judy. We'll stay in contact."

"I may be small, but I'm tough and determined. Harold should not be here, on our plain, doing these things. I will do some research and consult some other mediums and see if they have any suggestions."

Mel poured out more wine and, this time, Judy had a glass, as well. They were silent for a while. Iris thought that they were all, like her, in a state of shock. As Mike had said, there was no doubt that Harold's spirit was really around and interfering with their lives.

Judy and Mel left and Iris had a good cry afterwards. The shock had given way to emotion. Mike paced the room, muttering and clasping his head.

"Let's go to bed. We're both too upset to think properly. I'm going to go back to work tomorrow, I can't keep hiding from Harold. It will help take my mind off things as well."

"Okay. You're right. We've got Judy and Mel helping us now. Maybe we'll get together next week and have a brain storming session, if we haven't come up with anything by then."

"Thwarted for now, but I will be back." The words haunted Iris's thoughts. It didn't matter how often she turned them over in her mind, they made no sense. At some point she must have fallen asleep, but the next morning, the instant she awoke, the state of panic was back.

Chapter 25

Iris still took extra care when she was driving. The area in which she worked was still given a daily inspection. Knives and heat were treated with respect and a partial lowering of tension was achieved. Work was the distraction that was needed and any time not devoted to it, became time to ponder the problem.

"I think I've got something." Mike declared.

Iris sat down at the kitchen table and waited. She kept her face neutral. No excitement in case this went nowhere.

"Harold, as we know, blames the family for passing the flu to Edith. Could we find out, from the timeline we have, whether she caught it at the wedding, or if she may have got it somewhere else. If we could prove that this is wrong, maybe he will be forced to change his mind about taking vengeance on the Thomas family."

"So, check the timeline, have a look at medical sites and incubation periods."

"Yes, that's the sort of thing. After dinner we will hit the laptops and see what we can find out."

"The plan is to prove that he is wrong and then, with the help of Judy, call him back and explain it to him."

"I don't know if he will even listen, but we have to try something. Hopefully, we can prove, definitively, that he is wrong. If we can't do that, at the very least, we need to plant a seed of doubt."

"Let's give it a go. I think I'll give Judy a call at the weekend to see if she has anything to report. I can tell her what we're doing at the same time."

"Have you heard from Mel?"

"No. I think she is still in a state of shock. I'll leave her alone for a day or two. I wouldn't blame her if she backed away from this for a bit. We've confronted her with a ghost. A murderous ghost. She might not want to get further embroiled in it."

"She might need a couple of days, but I don't think Mel will back down. You are her best friend and she is going to do everything to keep you safe."

"I'm sure you're right, but I want it to be her decision."

"Fair enough."

The laptops were out again and the research began. Mike went back over his mother's notes. He needed the dates first and hoped that he would find them somewhere. He remembered a reference to Edith dying two weeks after the wedding, but was that a specific time, or did it mean, about two weeks. These details could be lost if they were passed down verbally.

He found Edith's death certificate, but there were no marriage certificates in the pile of documents. Iris was tasked with searching for that on line. She had signed up to one of the websites which helped one trace their ancestry and was finding it helpful in this instance.

It was Henry's marriage to Mabel where the contagion was supposed to have occurred. The date on the certificate that Iris found, was 10th June 1899.

"I've found it. 10th June 1899. How does that fit in with your death certificate?"

"Edith died on the 16th June 1899, less than a week later."

"Now we have to find out a bit about the flu to see how it all fits together."

Incubation periods, how quickly one died, Iris looked at these gruesome subjects. Reading the information, further lines of inquiry came up. Whilst people died of the flu, many died because the flu had exacerbated existing conditions. Edith was not the picture of health in the photograph and she had also just had a baby. What state was she in physically?

"What does the death certificate actually say? The cause of death, I mean." Iris asked.

"Bloody hell, I hadn't even looked at that. I was concentrating on the date. It says consumption and flu."

"That's tuberculosis, isn't it?"

"Yes. Where did the flu story come from? Why wasn't the consumption mentioned? That puts a whole new spin on it."

"Maybe there was a lot of flu around that year and they assumed that it was the reason she had died. I'm sure I can find some reference to that somewhere in a newspaper. Maybe there was an epidemic. I'm beginning to think that Harold was just a nasty man looking for an excuse to go on a killing spree. Maybe he was a psychopath, but didn't get to murder anyone when he was alive, so decided to make up for that in death."

"A lot of the evidence that we're going on is hearsay. Mum just took it as the truth. The whole story might be wrong. I don't know where we go now."

"We could ask Harold."

"As he has been quite happy to kill people, I don't think he would shy away from lying. It might take a bit more research. Back to the computers, then. See what we can find and, if we come up with nothing, we might have to ask him."

Why was it getting more complicated? What was the real reason behind Harold's deathly vendetta? How on earth did they find out the true story? Iris stared at the computer screen, hoping for inspiration and found none. She could do with some divine intervention. Never a believer, she said a silent prayer.

Chapter 26

Harold only had the example of his parent's marriage, on which to base his own. He came from a, middle class family, his father was the general manager of a large warehouse on the docks. A maid and a cook looked after the house, leaving his mother to manage her four children, issue orders, shop and take tea.

An accounts clerk did not earn a lot of money. Harold could not pay for two servants, new dresses for Edith and nights at the theatre.

"Things will get better, Edith. I'm due to be promoted to chief clerk in a couple of years and our lot will improve as a result."

It became obvious that his wife was not the type to undertake housework, having been coddled by her parents. Without his knowledge, and to his shame, Edith had gone to her father and said that they needed money. An allowance was paid each week, which was spent on a maid, who also undertook the cooking duties.

Edith's attempts at cooking had been poor. A diet of burnt meat and boiled potatoes was not going to maintain either of them. As much as Harold was embarrassed about having to accept help from his in-laws, his stomach was delighted. Fish and vegetables had been added to their bland menu.

The sea air and walking along the promenade had made Edith tired when they were on the holiday to the coast. Back home, she was still tired a lot of the time, despite not being particularly active. Her and Harold visited her parents each week, but she did little else. Visits to his family were less often. The house was often full of his siblings and their friends and his wife found it loud and exhausting.

At times, Harold found his circumstances were not to his liking. Edith did not even bother to get out of bed some days. There were compensations, though. The money from her family made their lives quite comfortable and she was a most lovely looking girl, with gentle manners and a soft voice. He had heard his mother harangue his father and that certainly wouldn't happen in his house.

The physical aspect of the marriage was not to his liking, either. Edith found the whole thing rather distasteful. Feeling ill and tired and having headaches were all excuses not to accommodate her husband's desires. At times she capitulated and he was grateful for that. More often would be better, but he would take what he could get.

The drift away from the rest of the Thomas family, was a gradual thing. For a while, after Edith had made it clear she did not enjoy going, Harold would visit on his own.

"Where's the lovely Edith, Harold?"

"She's swooning somewhere or shopping for another dress."

"Could she not manage to walk, on those spindly legs, from the front door to the cab?"

His siblings were merciless in their teasing. They patted him on the back and declared that they were only joking, but the barbs stuck. Much of what they were saying was too close to the truth.

A year after they were wed, Edith was pregnant. Harold had not been to see his family for a few months, but went to see them to give them the news. They were happy for him and congratulations came from every direction. A couple of, I didn't know you had it in you, comments were bandied about, but it was a good visit. As Edith took to her bed throughout her pregnancy, and was quite poorly, Harold stayed at home and cared for her. The tenuous bridge back to his relatives became lost once more.

As he watched his wife struggle with her growing belly, Harold was not sure that she would survive the birth of their child. Such a small, delicate woman and suffering from tuberculosis. How could she possibly deliver a baby? Simply getting out of bed made her tired. The approach of the birth brought more and more anxiety and dread.

Chapter 27

Mel called on Sunday afternoon and Iris was relieved to hear from her.

"Hi, Mel. I've been thinking about you, but I imagined you'd need a few days to get your head around the séance."

"I certainly did. I still can't quite believe any of it. We heard the voice and saw the mist, though. No way Judy could have conjured that up. It was for real."

"Pretty terrifying wasn't it."

"I was shaking afterwards. Then I thought about the threat to you and, well, I got home and had a good cry."

"I really appreciate you being there, but you don't have to get any more involved if you don't want to."

"Don't be daft. You're my best mate and I'll do whatever I can to help with this. It might just be pouring the wine, but that is important, too."

"Absolutely. I hoped you'd say that."

"Have you and Mike come up with any ideas about Harold? Have you seen him again?"

"No sign of him, thank God. We are trying to look back into Harold's past and see what started all of this. Mike's mum's research, said that his wife Edith died of the flu, but the death certificate says consumption, as well. TB to you and me. If we can find out the truth about her death, then maybe we can talk to him again and put our case. The problem is, finding out what happened back in 1899."

"I suppose there weren't the medical records like we have nowadays. Are there members of Mike's family that you can talk to? I know his mum spoke to some of them."

"She approached them in connection with the curse. I think that put some of them off. If I went about it, in a different way, I might get more success. See, already you've helped."

"Ian and I went out on Saturday night. It was one of his work colleague's birthdays, so we went to the pub. I was a bit quiet and he kept asking what was wrong. How would I even start to tell him? I feel bad that I'm hiding something from him, but he would think I was insane if I started talking about ghosts and things."

"That's a tricky one. Not many people believe in spirits and stuff like that. I know you really like him. Maybe telling him about it at this stage is not a good idea. It's something only you can judge. It's not a secret or anything, so if you want to tell him, it's not a problem."

"I might do a, bit by bit approach. Talk about you and Mike. Say that you've been looking into his ancestors and then work up to the fact that psycho Harold is killing people from beyond the grave and you are on his list."

"And hope that he doesn't run for the hills?"

"You know, I don't think he would. He is great and I like him a lot. Even if he thought I was totally batty, he would stick around and deal with it."

"We ought to do a night out. The four of us. I would love to meet him. Give him the best friend seal of approval."

"Oh, yes. I'd love that. I'll talk to him later and get something sorted. Are there any dates or times that you can't do?"

"No. Unless I'm dead, of course."

"DON'T, just don't. We are going to sort this. Have you worked out what Harold was talking about? The thwarted stuff."

"No. Mike and I have talked about it, but we haven't got a clue. Why did he have to be so cryptic? I hope he was referring to something specific, otherwise we might never know. He could just be messing with us."

"That yell, though. Old Harry was angry about something. We can only wait and hope to learn what he meant. It suggests that you might have some more time before he strikes. At least that's how I'm choosing to interpret it.

Stay positive. We will find something. Have you spoken to Judy?"

"Not yet, I'll call her later. Let's hope she has got something that can help us. I've got to keep the faith. With you lot on the case, how can I lose. Let's get that double date arranged. Maybe we can act like we're normal people, then when you reveal the ghost stuff to Ian, it won't seem so bad."

"We better not hit the wine too hard then."

"Agreed. Not that I've really fancied any. I think two nights in a row at the beginning of the week was enough. Mind you, in the circumstances it's not surprising I've been hitting it a bit hard."

"You've been back at work?"

"Yes. Went back the day after the séance. I needed something to occupy my mind. Still driving like a pensioner and checking my surroundings, but I feel a bit less tense now. At first, when all this started, I was scared. As time has gone on, I've got angry. It doesn't matter what happened with Edith in the past. Harold has no right to keep popping up and killing so many people. That's to say nothing of the suffering of those left behind. We've got to beat him."

"YES. If there's any thwarting to be done, team Iris is going to do it."

Iris felt better after talking to her friend. Mel always had a positive attitude and that was exactly what she needed right now. She smiled at Mike and he looked relieved. It had been a few days since they had found anything to be happy about. The phone call with Judy would wait until tomorrow. The high needed to be retained for the rest of the day.

Chapter 28

Judy had been able to talk to the dead since she was a child. Growing up with that talent, meant that she didn't get frightened by spirits. Not until she met Harold, that was. He was not like the people she usually called. The worst she had experienced, up until then, was a rather grumpy old lady who swore at her relatives. The fact that they were checking whether she had any more money stashed anywhere probably explained her attitude.

There was often a chill when someone appeared to her. A slight breeze or the twitch of a curtain. In old films, the table would shake and loud noises were heard, she had never known that. Not until Harold. A shiver ran through her as she thought about the séance she had done for Iris and Mike.

The air, on that occasion had been icy. Harold's approach had made her skin crawl. The light in the room seemed to dim when he arrived and Judy had to stop herself from crying out. She turned her fear into pity for the wretched Harold and her voice was steady when she had spoken to him.

Even as she had challenged him, Judy knew that he would not change or move on. Hate had anchored him to a place from which he could attack the living. Harsh words had been expected, but not the tantrum. Swirls of air, crockery being smashed, intimidation, he had tried a bit of everything. Then the extraordinary statement at the end. Thwarted, but he would be back. No one knew what that meant.

The hope, they had all expressed, is that Harold would leave Iris alone for a while. That would give them time to work out what to do. Judy was not sure what could be done about a spirit like this, so she would reach out to the community of mediums and invite suggestions.

She was a member of a sort of club. There was no title for the group, no fees, or membership rules. There was just a group of people, with the same gift as hers, who took their craft seriously. They contacted each other via messages and she composed a short essay giving the basic facts of the problem with Harold. Maybe someone would come up with a bright idea.

The first few replies were a bit sceptical.

"Has he really killed people?"

"You, say that people have seen him. In what form?"

"What evidence is there of these murders?"

"Are these deaths not just a coincidence?"

Judy answered them all with the details that Mike had supplied. Some took no further part in the conversation. Others were fascinated by the problem and saw it as a challenge. She was asked to describe the séance in detail and then the discussions started.

None of them had faced a spirit like Harold. They had encountered ghosts that did not want to move onto wherever, for a variety of reasons, but that did not cause a problem. How do you make someone leave? Particularly if they might be going to some sort of hell. The consensus was that they would have to give it some thought and then come back with ideas. Judy reminded them that they needed to work fast because a life was at stake.

Although Harold had not killed anyone outside of the Thomas family, Judy found herself being careful, like Iris had been doing. She drove a little slower and looked several times before she crossed a road. The spectre of Harold being angry with her and then taking some kind of revenge, stayed with her for a few days.

The group replied to her query with some dubious ideas. Many of them talked about doing some sort of exorcism. Judy was not keen on that, not being religious herself, and thought that approaching a priest with the story might get her locked up for being insane.

A veteran of the business, Clive, replied and made some interesting observations. All mediums had a talent. That talent was also a power. They could call someone to them and then dismiss them afterwards. That power might be the key to banishing Harold from where he now loitered.

It was a new concept and there was no guarantee that it would work. Judy had few options, so this would have to be looked into further. Rallying a number of people from the group would be the main problem. They lived all over the country and, some, had already said that they didn't want to be involved in an enterprise with a murderous ghost.

Iris would call at some point and at least Judy had a project

to present to her. She would try to sell it with enthusiasm,

but she wasn't convinced that it would work. Everyone she

had contacted had worried about venturing into uncharted

territory. She wouldn't back away though. Iris and Mike

needed her and she would do whatever she could to help.

Chapter 29

Judy had phoned other mediums and browsed the internet.

She had sent emails and messages and joined online

forums. Everyone who responded was interested in the

dilemma, but few had suggestions for how to deal with

Harold.

Mediums called spirits, conversed with them and passed on

messages. The proper ones did, of course, there were those

who were just faking it. Judy only discussed seances with

the ones who took the whole thing seriously and didn't see it as only a moneymaking enterprise. They had come up with the only suggestion of note.

Iris listened as Judy explained all of this.

"So, what was the suggestion that they came up with?"

"People like me have a gift. We can summon and we can dismiss spirits. Dismiss, but not move them onto another plane. It is speculation, because it has never been tried before, but perhaps enough of us could actually move him on. Combine our strength and eject him from the place he currently haunts."

"I've got to ask, Judy. What, if any, are the downsides to this? We know that Harold can hurt people. So far, he has stuck to the Thomas family, but he could lash out at anyone. I don't want you or one of your friends killed."

"There is an element of risk. If we manage to send him on, none of us need worry anymore. It is a theory at the moment. I think I need to get together with my friends and discuss it more fully. Explain how dangerous Harold is. We might even try banishing someone else to see if it's possible."

"That's an idea."

"It's quite exciting from my point of view. I know that we have to get on with this. There has been no indication when Harold might come after you, so we can't hang around. I'll round everyone up and have a meeting."

"I appreciate everything that you are doing, but you can't put yourself or any of your colleagues in danger. If you can manage to expel another spirit, we'll talk again. In the meantime, thank you for everything you are trying to do."

The conversation had taken place on speaker phone so that Mike could hear. They looked at each other afterwards and both wore frowns.

"I couldn't bear it if anyone got hurt trying to help me."

"I know. Judy has met Harold and is aware of the story. She can tell the others how real the risk is. It is up to them to decide if they want to try this."

"They are doing something. We are looking into Harold's story. At least we are trying to find a solution. We are in a better place than we were when this all started."

"Then there is Harold's "thwarted" thing. We don't know what that means yet. Whatever it was, he was furious about it. Anything that annoys him is fine by me."

Everyday, when Iris walked back into the house after a day at work, felt like a triumph. She was still alive. Things which she had done under sufferance, washing and cooking and cleaning, were now not so bad. She was still around and she was still doing them. What was the point of weeping and wailing. Fate would have its way.

The latest project for Mike and Iris was tracking down members of the Thomas family. Mike was still in contact with some of them. Cousins and aunts and uncles. The plan was to extend the search further. Iris had become proficient at searching the records on the ancestry site and was finding Thomas's spread far and wide.

"Have you thought about how we might approach them without mentioning the curse? We need to tease information out of them, rather than go in all guns blazing." Iris said.

"Let's see who mum actually spoke to. If we can find some who weren't part of her original enquiries, they won't have their guard up."

"Good idea. I'm grateful your mum kept so many notes of everything she had done. It must have occurred to her that we might need them at some time."

"Yes. I feel that I need to finish what she started. To save you, of course, but also for Becky and mum and dad. Not revenge. An ending to all the death. An end to the curse."

"Yes. It's about saving me, but also saving future generations and letting those that have already gone, rest in peace. Right. Let's carry on with the research. You look at your mum's records and I'll go back to the ancestry site. What we need is a dotty old aunt. Someone who will spill all the gossip."

"We'll be hard pressed to find anyone who knew Harold. When did he die, 1918. That means they would have to be around one hundred years old. Maybe aim for the generation after that. People who would have got the story before it became too diluted or changed with time."

"Then we work out the way to approach them. See, it's all so easy. Bish, bash, bosh."

"I like your optimism, Iris. Since when have you used the term "bish, bash, bosh."

"It seemed appropriate somehow."

Another smile exchanged. Each one meant so much more with impending death hanging over them. It was fleeting, though. Soon enough they were concentrating on their duties again. Iris jotted another name on the list and moved onto another branch of the family. How many of their relatives had died from the curse?

Chapter 30

Iris used her phone a lot nowadays. Checking in with Mike a few times a day, calling Mel every evening and speaking to Judy every few days. The conversation with Mel, always started the same. "Still Alive."

The weeks had passed rapidly since the séance and Iris was hanging in there. She hadn't seen Harold and that was a very good thing. A few names were on the list of Thomas family members to contact. The plan was to start calling them the next week. Not entirely sure what they were going to say, her and Mike were hoping that something would occur to them.

Another work day. Iris took her shower and made some toast. That morning, the thought of lashings of butter made her feel a little queasy. She managed to nibble at one slice and then gave up. Time to set out on the slow drive to work.

"Morning Iris. Ooh, you look a bit pale. Are you alright."

Wendy's observation made her retreat to the bathroom to inspect her face. The timing was fortuitous. She got there just in time, before she was sick. That had come out of the blue. Wendy was banging on the door asking if she was okay.

"Yes. I feel better now. I must have eaten something dodgy. I felt a bit off when I got up."

"You're not pregnant, are you?" Wendy laughed.

Iris denied the suggestion, quickly and then ruminated on the idea. As soon as lunch time came around, she would be heading for the chemist to buy a test kit. Dates, circumstances and that night of passion swirled in her head. There had been one bout of sickness. It was, surely, too soon to indicate anything.

The rest of the day, she was fine. The sickness had been in the morning. Wait. Wait until the test had been done and then think about the ramifications. The drive home was quicker, such was her need to get an answer.

Mike came home to find Iris sat at the kitchen table. Her expression could only be described as dazed.

"Are you alright?"

Iris waved the stick with the blue line at him. Taking it from her, he looked and understood. He flopped into the chair next to her.

"What does this mean? I know you're pregnant, but how does this factor into everything else. I know I should be ecstatic. I am ecstatic, but…"

"I know. Is this why Harold felt he was thwarted. Is he waiting to take our child at a later date. Is he waiting to take me at a later date. Neither of those things is acceptable and might just send me mad waiting for them to happen."

"The one thing this does give us is time. Harold prefers taking children, so that means that we have at least, what, eight months to find a solution to the problem."

Iris burst into tears. The options were all horrible.

"We're going to have a baby. A wonderful thing and all I can think about is when one of us will die. How long will he let me love my baby? I don't know which is worse. Seeing my child die or dying myself and never seeing it grow up."

"We are not going to let that happen."

The happiest day of their lives was turning into the worst day of their lives. Mike was so angry with Harold. He was a Thomas. He was the one that should die. How dare that miserable, dead, bastard come after his family.

"Do we tell people?" Mike asked.

"I need to tell Mel and Judy. Everybody else can wait for a while."

"Hang on a minute. I've got an idea. This is off the top of my head. Tell me if you think it's a bad one. We call relatives to tell them the good news about your pregnancy. We then segue into the bad luck others in the family have had. We won't ask a direct question, just allude to it. That might get some response."

"It's a way to start the conversation. I better practice saying the words, because every time I think pregnancy, I want to cry."

"This is a gift, Iris. A baby. It gives us time. It helps us approach the family and it will help us to win."

"If it's a boy, we are definitely NOT calling him Harold."

They didn't mention the child for the rest of the evening. Too many complicated scenarios and emotions were aroused when they thought about it. The news had to sink in and they had to make adjustments to their plans, hopes and dreams. They had to find the joy.

At home together, on a Friday evening, Mike and Iris had a chance to tentatively broach the subject of the baby. To her surprise, Mike placed his laptop in front of her and pointed at the cribs and prams that were for sale. He got a hug for that. It was time to get on with the business of having this baby.

There were people who needed to know about their news. Iris would visit her parents. She had paid quick calls in the last few weeks and they had guessed that something was not right. Their constant questions as to what was wrong had become more and more difficult to deflect. Now she could use the pregnancy as an excuse for being out of sorts.

Mel had to be told, and Judy, too, but that could wait until the next day. That night they would enjoy looking at, and talking about, baby things. Every day that they had their child would be precious.

Chapter 31

Mike was sat in front of the television, a newspaper, open, in front of him, but neither of these things could distract him from the amazing revelation from Iris. She was pregnant. His insistence that they never have children had been made with a specific worry in mind. Now, everything had changed.

As he had looked at the stripe on the stick, Mike had realised how much he actually wanted a family. The joy of that moment had been lost in the jumble of all the thought and fears that had followed. What did this mean with regards to Harold? Was this what was thwarting him? What would happen after Iris had the baby?

Mike wanted to tell the world, but he was terrified, too. Harold had threatened them and now they might only have their child for a short time. He couldn't help but think that Harold would leave Iris alone and wait to take their son or daughter. That was the cruel way his mind worked.

People talked about being in turmoil, but this was a step even beyond that. What emotion would sneak up and assault him next? Mike had been elated, then worried before he hit the depths of despair. He could not find the words to talk to Iris about what he was going through. He knew it would be similar for her. Not the same though. She had to carry this child for nine months. A mother and baby bond. How much harder it must be for her?

It took a few days for Mike to order his thoughts. It wasn't easy because he kept thinking about the haunted look that never left his mother after Becky had died. Iris could not suffer the same fate as her.

There had to be a way to stop Harold. None of the other murders had been committed with the victim having prior knowledge of their fate. They had been forewarned, thanks to his mother and that gave them a chance that no one else had. It was the twenty first century, for God's sake, and they would find the answer.

Mike wanted to say all of this to Iris. They had promised to be open with each other, but this subject was too difficult to tackle. He would find a way. When he had fully examined the situation, he would find a way to express how he felt. Which was?

Breaking it down, Mike thought back to his initial reaction. Delight. A glimpse of a child in Iris's arms, with him smiling at them. The love, the mess, the challenges and the laughter. That is what he had to hold onto. He must believe that good would triumph over evil.

Since his mother and father had died, Mike had thought about them, of course. He found himself talking to them, now.

"Mum, Dad, I've got some news. Iris, my wife, is pregnant. You are going to be grandparents."

They had never met Iris. Perhaps he should tell them a bit about her.

"You would love Iris. She's pretty and clever. Most of all she's kind. Kind, but with some steel in there somewhere. We are facing all kinds of problems, but she is so strong."

He took a breath and smiled at himself in the bathroom mirror. This was a bit mad, but somehow, necessary.

"Mum, sorry I didn't take much notice when you talked to me about the curse. Dad and I used to patronise you and think you had lost it. We were the stupid ones. Everything you said is true. Harold has come for either Iris or our baby. Don't worry, though, we are going to fight this in every way we can."

The chat had been good. Mike felt clearer about the future. They were having a baby and it was time to get on with it. What were they going to need? Mike had never thought that he would be a father and had no idea about what was involved. He had best start looking into it all.

A tentative search on his computer, brought up swathes of baby equipment. He had thought, pram and cot. It was a lot more complicated than that. Expensive, as well. Bottles, bottle cleaners, special this, special that. His mind was reeling. He didn't have to do this on his own. He had Iris. This was a problem to be solved together.

Chapter 32

"You look a bit happier, Chicken."

Iris had halted her father's usual escape to the garden and had made him join her, Mike and her mother in the kitchen for tea.

"At least get the biscuits out if you are going to stop me getting on with the potting."

Sue tutted at her husband, but got the biscuit tin anyway.

"Right. Are you settled down. I have some news."

Iris teased them for a while. Sipping her tea and selecting a sweet treat from the tin. Mike watched her with a grin on his face.

"Mike and I are having a baby."

Sue screeched and Tony clapped his hands together before loudly blowing his nose. Fierce hugs were followed by a great deal of sobbing from Sue and "well I never's" from Tony. Iris put the kettle on again and order was restored.

"I thought the idea was not to have children. Not that I'm complaining, far from it. I'm delighted that you have changed your minds. I might still have some baby stuff up in the loft. You'll have to have a look up there, Tony."

Sue was on a roll. She wanted her knitting patterns from the loft, too. A list was being prepared, of things that she would buy, and Tony was looking more stunned with every minute that passed.

Mike caught Tony's eye and gestured towards the back door. They made their escape whilst Sue was in full flow. Iris smiled at the exit and then revelled in her mother's plans. These were the moments that she needed to enjoy. Later she would talk to Mel. That would be interesting. For now, dissuading her mother from rushing to their house to redecorate the spare room as a nursery, was taking her full attention.

Mike and Iris left her parents in a buoyant mood. Their happiness and enthusiasm were infectious.

"Let's stop for a pub lunch. I know you can't drink, but it will be nice to treat ourselves."

"Oh, yes. I've been afraid to go anywhere except for work, and the supermarket. Going somewhere different will be great."

"Do you know what you are allowed to eat?" Mike asked as they perused the menus.

"I know absolutely nothing about being pregnant. I never thought it would happen to me. I will do a crash course in it when we get home. In the meantime, I'm sure that a burger and chips will be fine."

"And a nice glass of fizzy water?"

"Why not."

For a couple of hours, they felt like normal people. A married couple, enjoying a leisurely lunch. Smiling and laughing as they talked. Iris would remember this day. Lodge it in her memory, to be recalled when the spectre of Harold loomed and the fear returned.

Back home, Iris took her phone out of her bag and stared at it. Now, she needed to call Mel. It had been easy telling her parents. She knew what their reaction would be. With Mel it was different. She knew about Harold and the death threats and would immediately recognise all the jeopardy involved.

Make the call, she told herself, and the buttons were pushed.

"Iris, how are you doing?"

"Still alive."

"Any developments?"

"Yes. A most unexpected one. I'm pregnant."

"Oh my God, Iris, that's amazing… I think."

"I know all the things that are going through your mind at the moment. What does this mean with regard to Harold? I think we can safely say what is thwarting him now. What happens when the baby is born, well, that's not quite so certain."

"Will he still come for you? When it's born?"

"Maybe me. Maybe the child."

"Oh God. I've gone from so happy to so sad. I want to be auntie Mel. I want to share all the things you go through. How's Mike?"

"Feeling pretty much the same as us. I told my parents this morning. That was nice. They, obviously, don't know about the whole Harold thing, so it was lovely.

Grandparents to be, excited about it and elated for me and

Mike."

"That must have been good."

"It was, but then we leave there and it all comes crashing in

again. On a more positive note, this means that we have

about seven months to find a way to deal with our

murderous ghost. I'm going to tell Judy later. It will

hopefully give her a bit more time to work out what they

are going to do."

"The group banishment thing."

"Yes. I think it's a long shot, personally, but who knows.

Anyway, we're going to start calling some of Mike's

relatives tomorrow. See if we can get any information

about Harold and Edith."

"I'll be keeping everything crossed for you. Now tell me about this pregnancy thing. Was it intentional, or accidental?"

"Completely accidental. I was sick at work the other morning and, after a bit of denial, I got the test and there it was. The little blue line. I have been sick, a few times since and I'm finding it harder and harder to hide from the eagle eyed Wendy. I will tell her and the boss, but I want to get it all checked out first. I've got an appointment at the doctors next week to set the wheels in motion."

"I know it's going to be tough, but enjoy this, Iris. You're having a baby. The most wonderful thing that can happen. Enjoy it."

"I will, Mel. You'll be sick to death of all the baby talk in a few months. Pictures of the scan, discussions of names, complaints about swollen ankles. I could go on, but I haven't a clue what pregnancy is about."

Chapter 33

During the courtship and before the wedding, Harold had never heard reference to tuberculosis. He knew that Edith was delicate, but no specific ailment had been attributed to her ill health, as far as he knew. It was shortly after they had set up in their own home that the bombshell was dropped.

At a dinner with Edith's parents, her father drew him aside and revealed her diagnosis.

"I know that you will take care of our beloved daughter. She is as precious to you as she is to us."

"Of course, always." Harold replied.

"Her condition means that she is often tired, so the extra money we give you means that you can have a servant and give her treats occasionally."

"Her condition?"

"Yes. The tuberculosis."

The glare that emanated from Edith's father put a stop to any discussion. There was no chance for Harold to complain that he had known nothing about it.

As he examined the situation later, Harold realised that he had been conned. There had never been any talk of Edith having a serious illness. The truth had been hidden from him. It was partly his fault, because he had been blinded to anything beyond his wife's pale beauty. His siblings had joked about her being sickly and how right they were.

His in-laws knew that it would be difficult for their daughter to find a husband, when she was suffering from a life limiting disease. Edith had wanted to be married before her life ended and they had helped her to hook Harold without him having the full facts. Did that mean that he was just a convenient husband and not the man that his wife loved? So much had changed after that brief conversation with her father.

What did this mean for his future? What he knew about tuberculosis, or consumption, was not good. Those that were afflicted, grew weaker and then faded away. Sometimes they lingered for years. Was he to be the carer of an invalid wife, or a widower?

Edith's alabaster skin and tiny frame was the epitome of beauty at that time. He was still besotted with her, but he was angry at the circumstances he found himself in. Harold would never have a normal home life. His father-in -law had even had the cheek to caution him against having children. Was he meant to abstain from all contact with his own wife?

There had been so many clues about her illness. Weakness and coughing. The days when she had a slight fever. The reluctance to eat. Harold had compared her to Henry's fiancée Mabel and he had felt superior. Mabel was a robust, rather common woman and looked like a giantess against his elfin like wife. Only now, could he see how Mabel was, in fact, better than Edith.

The family couldn't know about her sickness, of course. They had made too many remarks about her already and a dozen, "I told you so" comments would only infuriate him further. For a while he took on a martyr like approach to the problem. He must do everything he could to make her life as good as possible. Even if that meant that he had to forgo certain things.

Edith had become pregnant. Quite remarkable really, considering her frailty. The bouts of tiredness before this event had been trying, but now she was almost permanently incapacitated. Harold's role as martyr was beginning to pall.

He began to work late some evenings. He had to work hard to earn that promotion, Harold explained to Edith. These were, actually, the evenings when, free from the responsibility of running around after his wife, he went and enjoyed himself.

Chapter 34

Iris spent a few hours immersed in everything antenatal. The basics, hospital appointments and scans, epidurals and gas and air, had permeated her brain, but there was a lot that she didn't know. There would likely be a pile of leaflets handed over by the doctor, but it didn't hurt to get ahead of the game.

Mike was wandering around with a soppy grin on his face. He was going to be a dad. That was not something he had ever believed would happen. Both of them paused and frowned, on occasion, but the mood was good. Seeing Tony and Sue's faces had helped. Sinking into his chair, Mike then thought about his own parents.

"It was great seeing your mum and dad so happy. I can't help but think about what mine would have said. Ignoring all the Harold stuff, I'm sure they would have reacted like your folks."

"Of course, they would. We'll have to make a scrapbook. Pictures of your mum and dad and of Becky, to show him the family he never knew."

"Show him? It's a boy, is it?"

"Well, I don't know, and I'll feel pretty silly if I'm wrong, but I think so."

"We better start thinking of a name for the son that will never be called Harold."

It was a couple of days later that Judy was informed of the latest development.

"I'm so pleased for you, Iris. This makes it even more important that we find an answer. It gives us time, too, which is good. "

The list of Thomas's was sat in front of them. The calls had been delayed again as they waited until Iris had seen the doctor. The excuse was that they wanted to ensure everything was okay before they broadcast the news. The names had been pored over and prioritised. Once they got the all clear, the contact could be started.

It would be interesting, if nothing else, to talk to members of Mike's family. They would be reconnecting with cousins and aunts and uncles, many times removed, who had probably never heard of them. A bit of explaining about how they were related would be the start of most conversations, they thought.

It had been a while since Iris had seen her doctor. She was fit and healthy and hadn't had anything more than a cold for years. The waiting room was full of the usual suspects. Older people, looking tired and anxious and young mothers with their babies. Schoolchildren coughing on everyone and teenagers fiddling with their phones. Checking her watch, the time of her appointment came and went.

"Iris Thomas?"

The doctor led her back to her room and then asked how she could help.

"I'm pregnant."

"Congratulations. I take it you have done the test?"

"Yes. Little blue line and all that."

"Okay. I'm going to take your blood pressure and some blood. Just normal checks. Is there anything that's concerning you?"

Iris smiled at that. Anything not worrying her would have been a better question.

"No. It was unexpected, but we are happy about it. I've had a bit of morning sickness, but nothing too terrible. I suppose I'm a bit unprepared, I don't know a lot about the process. Hospital appointments and all of that."

"I'll contact the hospital and set things going. Do you know how far along you are?"

"I think I'm about eight weeks."

"Okay, so you'll be having a scan pretty soon. People don't think about it, but it is worth checking your family history to see if there is anything hereditary which we should screen for."

"Oh. I was adopted. My mother died a few weeks after giving birth to me. I'm sure I can find out some details."

"Give it a try. It's better to know, but not essential."

"Thanks. Because she died, I've never looked into it any further. This will give me the impetus to learn a bit more about her."

Iris had always known that she was adopted. She knew for as long as she could remember. Although her parents had told her the basics, it was not a subject that had been discussed in any detail. It had been used as an accusation or an attack during her teenage years, but she had apologised afterwards. Her birth mother had died and there had seemed little point in trying to find out more.

It was a long overdue conversation. Iris wasn't sure that her parents knew much more about her mother, but they would have paperwork and it was worth looking into now.

She would call and see them one evening after work and talk to them.

"The doctor recommended that I find out a bit about my ancestry. Well, my mother's. My birth mother's. See if there are any hereditary problems. I'll pop in and see mum and dad after work, probably tomorrow, and speak to them. Apart from that, everything was straightforward. We'll get a date for the scan. Basically, we are now in the system, waiting for processing."

"You make it sound so exciting."

"Ha. The exciting bit is having a baby, Mike. Not all the other stuff that surrounds it."

"True. There won't be any problems talking to your folks about the adoption, then?"

"No. It's not something that we've gone into deeply. It never seemed necessary. It'll be good in a way, I think. A chat about it as grown ups will make it easier."

"Good. Do you need moral support, or are you going alone?"

"I'll go alone. You can get the dinner on for when I get home."

"Nicely manoeuvred, Mrs Thomas. Hope you like beans on toast."

Chapter 35

"Oh, Iris. What a lovely surprise. Come in. Tony, Iris is here."

"Hello, Chicken. How are you doing?"

"I'm fine, all is good. I went to the doctor's yesterday. Everything's fine, just went to say I was pregnant and get checked over. All pretty standard stuff. One thing she said got me thinking, though. She asked about hereditary problems. I suppose I better find out a bit more about my birth mother and look into it. I know I've got the birth certificate and adoption papers, but I thought you might be able to tell me more."

Sue and Tony exchanged a glance.

"We never talked to you about it, because you didn't ask. Your mother had died and that, kind of, stopped any further discussions." Sue said.

"I remember that I was told that she had died and that no one had come forward to claim me. Did she not have any other family members, or were they just not interested?"

"Your mother, Kate, had a mother and brother. The brother was much younger than her and the mother didn't want to take on a baby, even if it was her grandchild. She had a son of five and was not in a position to take you."

"There had been some sort of falling out between Kate and her mother, which complicated things." Tony added.

"Yes, that's right. I think other family members were found, but they were also estranged in some way from the mother, Vicky, and you were put up for adoption."

"What did my mother die of?"

Another look was exchanged.

"She drowned. There was lots of speculation about what happened. She had a cracked skull, which could have happened when she fell into the river." Sue patted Iris's hand as she told her.

"Or, she could have jumped, or she could have been pushed. Post-natal depression was mentioned. Also, your father disappeared from the area around the same time that she had died. There were lots of suspicions and not many answers."

"Wow. A lot to take in."

Sue was filling the kettle and reaching for the biscuits. Tony left the kitchen and headed upstairs.

"We kept some clippings from the papers about the investigation. There are a couple of pictures and bits and pieces. Your dad's gone to get the box. We didn't ever want to hide anything from you, but there was never a right time to dump all this on you. I suppose we thought that we were protecting you from a horrible story, which might affect your life."

Tony came back with a shoebox. Iris was disappointed that all the information about her mother was in such a small receptacle. After Mike's mother's box, she was reluctant to investigate this one in case it held more horrors.

"I'll look at it when I get home. Thanks dad. I totally understand why you didn't want to burden me with this. I'm a big girl now and I can deal with it. I might need a bit of time to get my head around it, but it's fine."

"What will you do now?" Tony asked.

"We've been looking into Mike's family, so I'd joined one of those websites that helps you find relatives. I'll start there, I think. There may be a time when I'll try to meet someone. My grandmother or my uncle. I'm not looking for a new family, though. I'm not expecting to have a lovely reunion with them and live happily ever after, they rejected me once, so why would it be different now. I'm after information that's all. Even though it doesn't need to be said, I'll do it anyway. You are my mum and dad. Always have been, always will be."

Iris took a chocolate biscuit and her dad frowned.

"Those are mine. I'll let you off, just this once."

His comment brought the smiles and laughs they all needed. Iris left with the box under her arm and strolled home.

"Perfect timing. I've only got the eggs to do and then I will serve up my speciality. Ham, egg and chips. How did it go with your parents?"

"Interesting."

Iris related the story to Mike and then they eyed the shoebox nervously. Lifting the lid, the meagre contents were revealed. There was a picture of her mother, Kate on top. The woman she saw was small with light brown hair. Sat in a park somewhere, she had a broad smile. It was all too much.

The tears carried on for a good hour. There were pauses whilst she ate her dinner and tidied up afterwards, but the emotion was never far away.

"I'd barely even thought about her. Knowing she was dead and that none of her family wanted me, I had no need to learn anything about her or her family. Then I see that picture and I want to know everything. What was she like?

Why did she fall out with her mother? How did she really die? Talk about cursed. It looks like my family are nearly as bad."

"The time is right, Iris. Like your mum and dad said, when was the best time to tell you? How would you have handled it all as a teenager? Now you need to know because of the baby and you are equipped, mentally and with the website, to look into it all."

"I love that you are always so practical and sensible, but it is annoying, too."

"You've stopped crying because you are amused that I'm annoying. I'll take that as a win."

Another set of people to investigate. Iris was pleased that she knew how the website worked. It would make this new search quicker than the first ones she had undertaken into the Thomas family. People went onto these sites to discover lost relatives and reveal pleasant surprises.

Everything she had done was because of tragedies past and yet to come.

The next thing on her to do list, was start making the calls to Mike's family. It couldn't wait any longer. Talk to a few people and see if she could get any information, and then she might have a chance to find out a bit more about Kate and her other family.

Chapter 36

"Hello, my name's Iris and I'm married to Michael Thomas, who we've learned is related to you. I'm pregnant and it's got us interested in other members of the family. I found you on one of those websites that helps one trace their ancestry and I'm gathering stories and family lore. It will be nice to be able to tell our child it's history."

This was the start to every conversation that Iris had that weekend, if she managed to get hold of anyone. They were all busy people leading busy lives. There had been a couple of promises that calls would be returned at a better time, but not much information. The best hope was that they would think about the call and then ring back, once they had some time to consider it.

Plenty of tea and coffee had helped her maintain the enthusiastic delivery, when she was rapidly running out of faith.

"Hello, my name's Iris…"

Another contact and, this time, she got someone chatty. Maggie was seventy-three, the right sort of age they were looking for. Iris sat up a little straighter and clicked her phone to speaker. Mike joined her at the table and they listened.

"Well, congratulations Iris. What a lovely idea. Which branch of the family are you from?"

"We started with Mike's great, great grandfather, Reginald. He had two brothers, Harold and Henry and a sister, Elizabeth. I traced from there and found lots of aunts and uncles, cousins and nieces and nephews. I thought I would contact the more, mature, family members because they are bound to have the best stories."

"My side is from a Charles. I know that Elizabeth's family ended up in Australia. We do the Christmas card thing, but I've never met any of them. I suppose you've heard of the curse?"

"Someone else I spoke to mentioned that. I noticed that there had been a number of deaths of children in the history, but that happened back then, didn't it."

"It would if it was childhood illnesses, but they were mainly accidents, or so I've been told. I have no evidence, as such, but there was talk."

"That sounds interesting. Tell me more?"

"Oh, not much to tell. Something about a miserable old relative who had cursed the family, hence all the accidents."

"Who was the relative?"

"It was Harold. Apparently, he was a nasty man and he wouldn't talk to any of the rest of the family."

"How do you know this?"

"My mother spoke about him. I think she kept a record of all the kids that died. She was quite superstitious. Liked all those fortune tellers and ghost stories. I don't know if any of it was true. The curse, I mean. It might have all been down to her imagination."

"You, said that she kept records. Have you still got anything. I'd made a note of some of the deaths and I'd like to compare my list to hers."

"Ooh, now you're asking. I'll have to dig around in the loft. Not personally, no way I'm that agile now, but one of my grandsons will do it for me if I ask. Leave it with me and I'll see if I can sort it out. You've got me curious, as well."

"Thank you, Maggie. I'm really glad I've had the chance to speak to you."

"We don't live too far apart. Maybe we could meet face to face. Have a coffee and a good gossip."

"I'd love that."

The call finished and Mike made tea.

"Nothing new from Maggie, but interesting, nonetheless." Iris summed it up.

"Yes, interesting. It seems that my mum was not the first person to start looking into Harold. I really hope that Maggie comes up with some records from her mother. Who knows what may be in them."

"We can't get excited about it. It might just be a list of names."

"You're right, but let's go with a bit of optimism, this time."

"I'm going to leave it there for today. End the calls on a good one. I will go and see Maggie at some time. She sounded like a lovely lady."

"Glass of wine? Small glass of wine? I keep forgetting that you have to be careful with alcohol. Making all those calls today, I thought you needed a reward."

"I do. A medium glass of wine, and I'll sip it slowly. Talking of drinking, I got a message from Mel. Her and Ian want to do a night out. Have something to eat, chat."

"Yes. We've not exactly got a full diary. Let's get it sorted. We could do with a change of scenery."

"Good. In that case, I'll go out and buy something new to wear. Everything is getting a bit tight around the waist."

"Are you going to buy one of those enormous smocks and some sensible shoes?"

"Er, no. I'm not really up on maternity fashion, but I think we have moved on from enveloping women in several yards of floral fabric. And whatever is on my body, heels will still be on my feet. When you're five feet, three, flats are not an option."

"Fair enough."

Chapter 37

"Okay. Let me get this straight. Your best friend, Iris, is being threatened by a serial killer ghost and you attended a séance, where he turned up and scared the bejesus out of you all."

"Yes. I know it sounds mad, Ian. Iris works in a post office, Mike is an accounts manager, they are not hippies. They don't dress in robes at the weekend and do pagan rituals. They are ordinary people who have been caught up in a bizarre situation. Having seen all the paperwork and heard Harold talk at that séance, I have no doubts that it is all true." Mel explained.

"The night my nan died, she came to visit me, even though she lived two hundred miles away. I swear she leant over my bed and said goodbye. She told me to be good. I was fifteen years old and had started hanging around with a gang of ruffians and I stopped after that. So, I'm open to spirits and the like. This is pretty extreme, though."

"Well, the medium, Judy, said that she had never come across a situation like it. She's trying to work on some plan to get him, Harold, banished back to wherever he should be. I wanted to tell you all of this before you met them. It's the most pressing thing in their lives, and mine, at the moment and something about it is bound to come up on Saturday."

"I get it. I'm not going to take the mickey, or anything like that. It's important to you, so it's important to me."

"Thank you, Ian. I knew you'd understand."

Iris and Mike arrived at the Italian restaurant and saw Mel and Ian waving at them from a table near the back.

Mel's boyfriends were usually, good looking rogues. Ian was different. He was an attractive man, but not one of those flash types who had probably spent an hour doing their hair. Iris liked the look of him immediately.

Introductions were made and drinks were ordered. A good start to the evening.

"I'm going to address the elephant in the room. I told Ian about Harold. I talked about the curse and the séance, so, he is up to date on all things ghostly." Mel said.

"Well, you're still here, Ian, so that's good. We don't expect you to believe it, as it's one hell of a story." Mike added.

"You're right. It is hard to believe, but as I said to Mel, I've had my own, albeit less threatening, ghost experience, so I'm not dismissing it. She's on board with trying to help you with this in any way, so count me in."

An audible sigh was heard from all present and the evening could progress in a lighter mood. Mel and Iris exchanged a smile and a nod. Ian had earned the seal of approval within minutes of being introduced.

The conversation ebbed and flowed, jobs, food, holidays, family, but always came back to Harold. Ian was the one that kept drawing them back. He had a need to understand more about the curse and why everyone believed that a spirit could cause so much death.

"Next week, one evening, come around to our place. Mel and Iris can gossip, they're good at that, and I'll show you the paperwork. We've got death certificates and press clippings, as well as all my mum's research. I think you will get a better idea of it all if I show you. You don't have to do that, but you seem interested, so the offer is there."

"Yes, I'd like that. It's a mystery and I want to learn more about it. A fresh set of eyes might see something that can help, as well. And if there's another séance, I definitely want to be there."

"You might regret that, Ian. The last one ended with what can only be described as a mini tornado in our kitchen. Crockery smashing, Mel screaming and me shrieking."

"Sounds quite exciting, Iris."

"It certainly was."

The night came to an end and when Iris and Mike got home, they discussed the events.

"I think Ian has the thumbs up from both of us." Iris said.

"Yes, definitely. Fair play to him for embracing the whole Harold thing."

"Well, it is fascinating isn't it. The more we all learn about it, the better. Like he said, fresh eyes and all of that. So, they're coming around on Thursday. Do we need to feed them?"

"Oh, I'm not sure."

"I'll message Mel and check. I'm glad that we get on so well with Ian. I need to see as much of Mel as possible. I don't know how much longer I'll be around."

Most of the time, Iris was successful at putting thoughts of impending death to the back of her mind. Then, all of a sudden, something made her think about it again. Each mention was supposed to inure her to it, but it was just as difficult to say for the tenth time, as it had been for the first.

Did Harold listen in on their conversations? Was he revelling in the pain that he was bringing to their lives? Iris resolved to not speak her fears out loud any more. She had to live the best life that she could and deprive Harold of his fun.

Chapter 38

The scan would be soon and then Iris would tell her work colleagues about her pregnancy. She would have to order a new uniform as well, to accommodate her growing waistline. Wendy had looked her up and down a couple of times and it was getting harder to keep it quiet.

Iris took a stroll in her lunch hour most days. A chance to stretch her legs and look in shop windows. The clothes in the window of the chain store, were skimpy and tight. Two things that were entirely inappropriate for her circumstances. She would go in anyway, on the off chance that they had anything that would fit her.

Clasping a bag which contained a loose, silky blouse, Iris left the shop and turned towards the post office. Face to face with her was a youth. The same youth, who, a few months ago, had waved a knife in her face and demanded her phone. He showed no glimmer of recognition, a blank stare, but she knew him.

The boy stepped to the side to go around her, but she moved, too and blocked his way. He moved back in the other direction and once more she was in front of him.

"Scuse" he managed.

"You don't remember me? The lady you and your little mate tried to mug a couple of months ago."

The lad was now bright red and looking for an escape.

"Wait. I just want to ask you something. That night, you saw something that scared you and then the two of you ran off. What did you see? When I turned around there was nothing there."

"Shit. I remember. It was a ghost."

"What did it look like?"

"It was a shape, like a man, yeah. It pointed at Dean and then at me and then its mouth opened in, like a scream, but there was no sound."

"Like a man. Did you see any features. A nose or eyes. Did it have a moustache?"

"What? This is freaking me out all over again. Yes, it had a moustache. How would you even know that?"

"Never mind. I just needed to know what you saw. By the way, I'm glad it scared the shit out of you."

"Thanks lady. I'll have those nightmares again now."

Iris walked away leaving the lad shaking his head as he left in the opposite direction. God, she wished she had seen Harold. He showed himself to strangers, but to the people he murdered, he was just a mist.

Wendy demanded to see what was in the bag when she got back.

"Nice colour. I love green. Big, though. And baggy. Anything you want to tell me?"

"Yes, I'm pregnant. I was going to tell you and the boss once I had my scan, but there was no hiding it from you. Keep it to yourself for a couple of weeks and then I'll make the announcement and you can look, suitably, surprised."

"I'm so pleased for you and Mike. All that, I'm never having a baby, stuff. I was fairly sure you two would change your minds at some point. You'll be a great mum. You're so patient and kind…"

Wendy had to stop because Iris was crying.

"I'm sorry. The hormones are getting to me, I think."

"I understand. Went through it myself. Come here."

Iris was given a bear hug and it felt good. Bloody Harold and his constant menace. He had made her cry again.

It was nice that Wendy knew about the baby. Extra cups of tea appeared and she took any lifting job without complaint. Harold would have to be brave to attack her at work with Wendy looking after her.

That evening, Mike listened to her story of meeting the potential mugger and his description of the ghost he had seen.

"First, what were you doing confronting your mugger on the high street."

"He was the one who followed orders, not the main man. He wasn't going to start anything without his mate. Anyway, my need to know what he saw, outweighed anything else. And secondly?"

"Yes, secondly, how confused was that kid when you asked him if the ghost had a moustache."

"It was quite funny, now I think back on it. He said that he was going to start having nightmares again. I don't feel sorry for him in the least. Maybe it will make him rethink his life of crime. Oh, and Wendy made me tell her about the pregnancy."

"Made you?"

"She had guessed and confronted me. It was difficult telling someone else who doesn't know all about the other stuff. I burst into tears. It reminds me what might be in our future. I blamed it on my hormones and she was fine."

Each person that learned the news, made it more real. Already twelve weeks pregnant and that meant that their time was ebbing away. The need to contact more members of Mike's family was pressing, but Iris needed to find out about her own family, too. Armed with her birth certificate and the adoption paperwork, there was enough information to get started.

Katherine Warren. Her mother's name was typed into the computer and the search began. Immediately, Kate's mother Victoria was found. The woman who had rejected her when her mother died. She would have to try to talk to her, however unwelcome she might be.

Chapter 39

Harold sat in the drawing room whilst the wails from the bedroom rang out around the house. The doctor was upstairs, with a nurse, tending to Edith and he was with her parents. They had been at the house every day for the last three weeks, waiting for their daughter to go into labour.

Edith's father wore a permanent scowl, furious that his daughter was being subjected to the rigours of childbirth. Harold had not been well liked by his father-in-law and he was now loathed. Another scream and Edith's mother began to pray.

Hours passed and still the cries came. They were getting quieter and that was troubling. Harold was frozen in his chair. Guilt for putting Edith through this torture weighed on him and the glares from her father compounded his misery.

What would he do if she died? The longer it went on, the more likely it seemed that this would be the outcome. He thought that his father-in-law might physically attack him if it happened. An almighty shriek was followed by the cry of a baby. They all jumped to their feet and rushed to the bottom of the stairs.

They were waiting again. At last, the doctor appeared and descended slowly. He looked exhausted and they wondered what news he was about to deliver. His face was a mask of fatigue and unreadable.

"You have a son, Mr Thomas."

"What about Edith?" her father asked.

"Yes, how is my wife?"

"It was difficult. She is so tiny, and not in the best health. The birth took a lot out of her and it will take time for her to recover, but she is not in any danger. I will, of course, visit her each day until I'm satisfied with her progress. The nurse is cleaning the child and seeing to Mrs Thomas and then she will be ready to see you."

The comments were addressed to Harold, but it was her father who got into the room first, when they were finally admitted.

Edith was as white as the sheets upon which she lay. Her mouth was open as she took small breaths. Harold thought that she looked like she might expire at any moment. His son was now in her mother's arms and he had still not got near him.

"I'd like to see my son, now."

A loud, slow tone made them all stop and look. The boy was thrust at him and he gathered him into his arms. Dark hair and blue eyes. He was a Thomas.

Everyone was ushered from the room and Edith was left to rest. It would be many days before she got out of bed again. The baby was taken to her to coo over and as soon as he cried, she handed him back. Bertie Thomas was a good baby. He was fed by bottle as his mother was unable, or unwilling, to feed him herself. Harold found himself doing many things that other fathers would not even consider doing.

The maid helped and his mother-in-law did some things, but she, too, was squeamish about the more unsavoury tasks. Edith's father only visited when Harold was at work. They had little to say to each other after their last exchange. Harold had been told that he was not to make Edith pregnant again.

There was little chance of that. Every encounter had been submitted to reluctantly and, once she was pregnant, Edith had spurned all of Harold's advances. Bar some kind of miracle, she was not going to conceive. A new baby, a sickly wife and enforced celibacy. This was not married bliss.

Harold did what many others in similar circumstances did. He sought the pleasures of the flesh elsewhere. Not some sordid fumble in an alley. He went to a house where the services were on offer. A little more expensive, but it amused him to think that he was spending Edith's father's money on prostitutes.

It was these nights that kept him going. It gave him a way to live in, what had become, a loveless marriage. Were it not for his son and the allowance from Edith's family, Harold might have simply packed his bags and left. He could quite happily live without seeing Edith or her family again, but he could not live without seeing Bertie.

Congratulations had come by telegram and letter from his family. They did not ask to come and see the baby and he did not invite them. News that his brother Henry and Mabel were getting married, made him agree to attend and bring Edith and Bertie. The child was bonny and his wife was not so frail. The offer of a new dress roused her from her bed and she went shopping with her mother. Whilst they were out, he visited his favourite girl, Lottie. He took his pleasure where he could.

Chapter 40

Victoria Warren had married again and was now Victoria O'Neill. She lived about twenty miles from Iris and Mike's house. There was a dilemma about what to do next. Should Iris call her and arrange a meeting, or just turn up there, If, she phoned and was then rejected, her chance was gone.

The uncle had been traced, too. He was fathered by a man who was shoe horned in between Kate's father and Vicky's present husband. Carl Parker was thirty-three years old and lived a few streets away from his mother. He was only five when Kate died and probably had little recollection of his sister. It was vital, therefore to see Vicky.

Mike and her discussed the pros and cons of turning up on the doorstep. It wasn't ideal, but they felt there was no choice. They set off on a Sunday morning with the hope that they would find someone at home.

The house that they approached was a terraced home with a neat front garden. By her calculations, Iris thought that Vicky would be about seventy. The short path to the front door seemed a mile long. Mike grasped her hand as they stood at the door and then she pressed the bell.

Vicky stood before them. A similar height to Iris, her hair was grey and she had a slight frame. They were definitely from the same family. There was no subtle way to do this, so she dived straight in.

"Hello. I'm your granddaughter Iris."

A sigh escaped from Vicky. It took her a moment to collect herself.

"Yes, I can see that. You look like your mum. Come in. We don't want to be sobbing on the doorstep."

They were introduced to Vicky's husband Jeff, who was aware of the story, and greeted them warmly. He went to make tea and they sat in the lounge, dabbing the tears from their eyes.

"If you don't mind, Iris, I'd like to tell you about your adoption. There are things I need to get off my chest. Afterwards, we can discuss other stuff. I'll give Carl a ring, too and you can meet your uncle."

"Yes, please go ahead."

"Kate was pretty, like you. There were always lots of boys hanging around her. I was a mother at twenty-two and I hoped that she would wait until she was older, but it was not to be. The main problem, and I don't discount my role in all of this, was my partner at the time. Carl's father, Jim. I'd been divorced for a few years and he came into my life when I was struggling with money as a single parent.

"Him and Kate never got on. She was at that age, thirteen, where she was awkward and he was not an easy man. Then I became pregnant and things got more difficult. Jim liked his drink. There were rows and the odd slap. Kate hated him and couldn't wait to leave home. At eighteen she was gone and living with some guy who was thirty. We were angry with each other. She was furious that I let Jim walk all over me, but I had Carl and couldn't cope without him. I was angry that she had tried to come between me and Jim, although, deep down, I understood, I couldn't let her interfere.

"She got pregnant. Your dad's name was Hugh Forsyth. His family had a few quid. Kate was young and pretty and he liked having her on his arm. A baby, though, that was not for him. He disappeared not long after you were born. Do you know about what happened to your mum?"

"My parents, adoptive parents, told me some of it. The speculation about how she died."

"I don't know what happened. Hugh vanished around the time that she died. She was a teenager trying to cope with a baby. Who knows. Anyway, they came to me to see if I would take you, which I wanted to do, but Jim wouldn't have it, so you went for adoption.

"Should I have insisted that I was, having you? We could debate that for hours. As it was, a couple of years later, after being punched by him one time too many, I finally ditched Jim. It was too late by then to do anything. You were with your new family and they seemed like good people. I thought it best to keep out of your life and let you decide if you wanted to find me and Carl. I thought about you a lot over the years and I'm glad that you are here."

A further bout of crying followed. A toilet roll was produced when they had used up all the tissues.

"All I knew about my family, was that my mum had died and that no one wanted me. My adoptive parents are wonderful people. I knew from a young age that I was adopted, but they could never find the right time to address the way Kate died and, as long as I didn't ask, they didn't tell. Recently, I've found out I'm pregnant and that has been the catalyst for finding out more."

"Oh, my God. Are you telling me that I'm going to be a great grandmother."

"Yes."

It was strange and a bit awkward at times, but the meeting was a success. Uncle Carl arrived and he was pretty emotional, too. He took after his father, Iris suspected, as he was a large, dark haired, man.

Jim, the cause of so much turmoil in Vicky's and her mother's lives, had moved on. Carl hadn't seen him since he was eight years old. He remembered only the shouting and the violence and had no desire to see him again. His memories of Kate were better.

"She was good to me. She would read me stories and come to my room and sit with me when Mum and Jim were arguing. I cried a lot when she left and then a whole lot more when we found out that she had died."

"I hope we can keep in contact." Vicky said.

"Yes. I would like that. I know it was a bit of a shock us turning up today, but I couldn't risk you saying no to a meeting. When we get together again, we can plan it better. Hopefully there will be less crying, too."

Hugs and goodbyes lasted a while and Carl, Vicky and Jeff, were still waving as they drove away.

Chapter 41

There wasn't much conversation on the journey home. Iris was shell shocked by the whole experience. One minute, she was an adopted only child and now she had a grandmother and an uncle. There were probably other family members, too, but that was enough to be going on with.

At home, with a cuppa in front of them, the analysis could begin.

"Well, that went a lot better than I'd expected."

"I was worried about it, Iris. There might have been no one home, or an ugly confrontation on the doorstep. I'm relieved that neither of those things happened."

"It's about time we had a bit of luck. I had a good feeling about today. I didn't say anything, because you would think I was mad, but it was okay. Seeing her on the doorstep was the first of a number of OMG moments. Having seen the picture of Kate, I knew it was her right away. She was petite and had the same features."

"Like you."

"Yes. I knew there would be a story. Why she hadn't taken me when Kate died. I've never dwelt on it, but knowing that I was alone in the world, apart from my mum and dad, did have an effect on me. I don't know what I would have felt if I thought they were around but rejected me. That would be worse, I think. Anyway, now we know the other side of the story. Jim sounds like a, thoroughly unpleasant man."

"It's that coercive control. He wouldn't let Vicky take you, even though she wanted to. It would have ben hard for her, if she had. She would have ended up as a single parent with you and Carl. I think you being adopted was the right thing at the time."

"You're right. I wouldn't want to be without Tony and Sue. They have been wonderful. I'll tell them about this meeting. I'll reassure them, as well, that no one can ever take their place."

"They know that."

"As a first meeting, I'm happy. We've only scratched the surface, of course. Now that we are not with Vicky, I can think of a million things that I want to ask. About Kate growing up. About my dad. All the little things, like favourite foods and pets. What music did she like, stuff like that. The big question is about her death. We only touched on that today."

"You and Vicky might be related, but you are strangers. You need to get to know each other a bit better before you broach the tricky stuff."

"Jeff was nice. I'm glad that she found a lovely man after the hell Jim put her through."

"There was no mention of other grandkids. I take it that Carl isn't married."

"I never even thought to ask about that. I'm sure they would have mentioned it. I'm presuming he looks like his father. Nothing petite about him was there."

"Ha, no. Hulking great man. Luckily, he seems to have inherited his mother's nature. Sounds like your father was quite well off. Maybe hit him up for twenty-eight years of pocket money that you missed."

"A grandmother and an uncle are enough for one day. I'm not sure about Hugh Forsyth. He seems to have been one of those rich, feckless, types. He certainly didn't hang around when Kate got pregnant. I wonder if he ever saw me. As a baby, I mean. Did he pop into the maternity ward with a bunch of flowers and then say "Right, I'm off".

"One day, you might want to ask him that, but, as you say, two new relatives are enough to be getting on with."

"My mind is racing, now. Horrible Harold is someone we could do without, but he has certainly set the ball rolling. We are happier, I'm pregnant ad I've met members of my family. We have also made contact with members of your family that you haven't spoken to in years. I can't help but think that this is all happening for a reason.

"Don't look at me like that. I'm going to be a mother. We are all filled with intuition and wise sayings. It happens automatically when you get pregnant. I could probably teach Judy a thing or two."

"Okay, wise other to be, what are we having for dinner tonight?"

"I hadn't even thought about that. Today has been too exciting for mundane things like cooking."

"Let's nip into town. I'm sure they do a roast at the gastropub. A bit of a treat to round off the day."

"Now you're talking."

Chapter 42

Mel arrived with Ian. The men decamped to the lounge and the girls sat at the kitchen table. In solidarity with her friend, Mel was drinking tea rather than wine.

"What a day. Meeting your grandmother and your uncle."

"It was more than I could ever have hoped for. There was an explanation about why they didn't take me and that was a huge help. There's a lot more to find out, but that will come in time. We are definitely going to keep in touch and they are excited about the baby."

"Your grandmother?"

"Vicky."

"Yes, Vicky. She couldn't throw any light on what happened to your mum?"

"No. That remains a mystery, for now. I think she knew more, but I was a stranger turning up asking questions. Hopefully, next time we meet, she will tell me more.."

"Will you try to find your dad?"

"I've thought about it, but if he's not a murderer, he is, at the least, an unpleasant man who abandoned Kate when she had a baby. He's not a priority. I think I'll go back further into my family, though. See who came before

Vicky. I've got quite into this whole ancestry thing."

"Have you had a look at Hugh? On the internet, I mean."

"No, I haven't. Let's see what we can find."

The laptop was plugged in, chairs were arranged and the

name, Hugh Forsyth, was entered into the search engine.

A few newspaper stories came up. Two were about the

death of Iris's mother. He had been questioned by the

police about the young mother's death. He had stated that

he had not abandoned his child, he had been told to leave

by Kate. She had said that she planned to raise the child on

her own. He was not the type to settle down and she had

recognised this.

So much for not being the type to settle down. Another

article, in a posh magazine, featured Hugh and his wife and

two sons. They were stood outside their manor house.

There was an interview, in which he talked about his latest

business venture. He was importing exotic vegetables from somewhere in Africa.

"You've got two brothers, as well. Your family is growing rapidly."

They pored over the picture of Hugh. Enlarging it on the screen to get a better look.

"He has that look. You know. Rich, but kind of useless." Iris said.

Hugh had sandy blond hair, swept back in a sort of bouffant quiff. He was wearing jeans and a shirt and waistcoat. His wife was a glamourous woman with long honey coloured hair. The boys looked sweet and were around ten years old. The magazine was dated ten years ago. Her half-brothers were now in their late teens or early twenties. Iris wondered what reception she would get if she turned up on Hugh's doorstep.

She could see how the dashing Hugh had turned her mother's head. An older man with money. He almost certainly had some type of flash car and bought her clothes. Underwear. Red underwear. That's what he would have bought.

The last picture they found was from a year before. Hugh still had the quiff and the waistcoat and was promoting his goat's cheese business. No mention of the exotic vegetables.

"He seems to be desperately clinging onto youth. Look at those boots with the Cuban heels. Wonder what he would say if he found out he was about to be a grandfather." Mel laughed.

"I can't see any mention of his wife and kids in this article. He was likely caught having an affair with some younger woman."

"Yes, he looks the type."

"I see the pictures and it makes me curious, Mel. I don't think that he would be pleased to see me though. Especially if he had something to do with my mum's death. We've still got other priorities as well. A certain ghost who is threatening me. I think I should devote my time to that problem first, and then worry about Hugh later."

"Shall we check on those boys? See how freaked out Ian is after seeing all the notes about Harold."

There were pieces of paper spread everywhere. Mike and Ian were currently flicking through the photo album, putting names to the faces they had been talking about.

"What do you think, Ian?" Iris asked.

"What a story. All the strange ways that people died. The ghostly appearances. And then the séance. I've got to admit, I'm more inclined to believe it all now. It's fascinating, but awful, too. I can't imagine the pressure you two are under. This has given me a lot to think about."

"You look like a man who needs a brandy. What do you say Ian?" Mike offered.

"I say, yes."

"What about you two? Can I get you anything? Glass of wine, Mel?"

"Oh, go on then. Just a small one. I'm driving."

"It was a good evening then? Your chat with Ian."

Iris and Mike talked about their visitors.

"Yes. He's a nice bloke. He got into the whole thing. Looking at the notes and paperwork, listening to the tales. He kept saying that he wanted to do something to help. I suspect you and Mel were talking about your new found family."

"Yes, we were. We looked up my dad, too. Hang on and I'll get my computer."

Mike looked at the pictures and read the articles. He saw the photo of the two boys, who were Iris's half-brothers.

"Maybe you can avoid Hugh, but meet your brothers."

"That would be the ideal situation. As I said to Mel, though, that has to wait. We have Harold to deal with before then."

"The scan is the next thing. We can, hopefully, find out if your assertion that it's a boy is correct and then do the rounds and tell everybody. Then we have to think of a suitable name and buy lots of blue things."

Chapter 43

Iris had connected with lost family. A wonderful thing. How long would she have to get to know her grandmother and uncle? A couple of pictures had been taken when they were at Vicky's and she kept looking at them. Sitting next to her phone was the photo of her mother, Kate. Grandmother, mother and daughter were very similar.

All of the females were small and slim. They all had light brown hair. Iris was blonder, but only with chemical help. The picture of her father Hugh, was also examined occasionally. She couldn't see his genes in her. His hair was fair, but he was tall and willowy. Her stature was definitely from her mother's side.

Then there was Carl. He was totally different. Iris had found some information on Jim Parker, her grandmother's former partner and Carl's father. The internet had revealed that Jim was arrested in a domestic violence case a couple of years after his break from Vicky. The newspaper article had a picture and Iris was able to see the thug who had influenced her life.

Jim was squeezed into a suit for his court appearance, in the photograph. He was an average guy. There was no way of looking at him and thinking that he was capable of hitting a woman. Vicky was probably charmed, wined and dined before the dominance and coercive behaviour kicked in.

The whole scenario was riddled with what ifs. The presence of Jim stopped Iris being adopted by her grandmother. That, of course, would mean that she would never have become part of Sue and Tony's family. She wouldn't have wanted that. The big regret was that she hadn't learned more about her mother. At least that could be rectified, now.

Thoughts had gone around in Iris's head, and now she was back to how much time she might have with Vicky and Carl. There could be no delay. She would have to arrange another meeting with her grandmother as soon as possible, because there was a lot that she wanted to know.

There were more people from Mike's family to contact and Iris had to change her focus and concentrate on that.

"Hello, my name is Iris and I'm married to Michael Thomas." The calls began again. It was like cold calling people and trying to sell them double glazing. Iris was met with suspicion or indifference. The nearest that she had got to a positive response was when a cousin, many times removed, said that they had a box of old papers relating to the family. Iris had put £10 into their bank account to pay for it to be sent to them.

"That's it. I'm going to call it a day. We've got a box of papers coming, but nothing else of note."

"I wonder what will be in the box?" Mike said.

"Either a complete history of the family from medieval times or some recipes from an ancient aunt."

"Two possibilities, but more likely is old bills that haven't been paid."

"Or bank statements which show a balance of ten pence for the last five years. NOT share certificates that are worth a fortune."

"Have you spoken to Vicky yet? Give her a ring and meet up. I know you are desperate to learn more about your mother. You better report into Sue and Tony, too. They will be anxious to know how you got on with the information they gave you."

"I'll visit my parents in the morning. I'll go alone. I don't want them to feel awkward talking about all of this. Once I've seen them, I'll call Vicky. The temptation is to spend a lot of time with her, but I mustn't neglect my other family in the process."

The visit to her parents started in the usual manner.

"Iris. Let me get you some tea. How are you? Are you hungry?"

Sue and Tony were staring at their daughter trying to read her mind.

"Let's sit down with some tea and I'll tell you all about my visit to Vicky."

"Oh, you went to see her."

"Yes, and it was fine."

The meeting was related, from the knock, on Vicky's front door, to the tearful departure.

"We never knew the reason that she never took you. There wasn't any direct conversation between us and her. It was all second hand through social works and the like. We wanted you. We got you, and nothing else mattered."

"Like your mum says, we didn't want to ask more questions and rock the boat. Did you learn anything more about what happened to your mother? Your birth mother."

"No. Vicky said she didn't know. She had only just met me, though. Perhaps she was reluctant to reveal too much until she knew me better. I hope so, anyway. I need to find out more about Kate. What she was like. I saw the photo of her in the shoe box and it provoked a lot of emotions. I need to do this. I never thought that my other family was important, but it is. You do understand, don't you?"

"Of course, we do. Sue and I have talked a lot about it over the years and especially in the last week. It's natural for you to want to know about them. I'm relieved that you've met them and that you get on well. You never know how these things are going to turn out."

"She looks like me. My mum I mean. Vicky does, too. Or, I look like them. I've looked up my dad, as well. He's a bit of a rogue, I think. I've no great desire to meet him, but that might change at some point. For now, I've got quite a lot to be going on with."

Chapter 44

Iris was sat with Vicky at her house. As this was an arranged meeting, there had been more time to prepare. Photo albums and school reports were on the table and, as they went through them, the story of her mother's life was being told.

"That could be me. How old was Kate there?"

"I think she was eight. She was so skinny, but she had a big appetite. Were you the same?"

"Yes. I had those same thin legs. I was a bit of a tomboy when I was that age and it looks like she was, too. It's so good seeing all these old photos. Thank you so much, Vicky."

"I knew you would want to see them. You're bound to be full of questions. It's so sad that her life was short and there is not much to tell. If you think of anything else you need to know about, just call. I've told you a few anecdotes, but I'll think of more. I like to think of her younger years. Full of energy and cheeky with it. That sulky teenage stage coinciding with Jim was the perfect storm. Part of me was gutted when she left, but part of me was relieved. I thought that Jim would end up hurting her."

"Did you know my dad?"

"I met him a couple of times. Very suave and handsome. He was, what's the word, all talk, but nothing solid about him."

"Superficial?"

"Yes, exactly. He had money from the family, but no real job. I tried to tell Kate that he would soon be off to the next pretty young thing, but she wasn't having it. We weren't getting on well at that stage and she wasn't going to believe anything I said."

"I looked him up on the internet. I wanted to know what he looked like. I'm not sure that I'll ever try to meet him. All the rumours around Kate's death. Do you think he had something to do with it?"

"He struck me as a bit of a weed. He could use the nasty words, but I don't think he had it in him to do any violence. Kate was gutted after he left. She said that he had been cruel. I couldn't help much with looking after you. Jim didn't want Kate or you in the house and I had hardly any money myself, so I couldn't help that way either. It breaks my heart to say it, but I always thought she had committed suicide. Alone with a baby. Living in a hostel and no money. It must have seemed hopeless."

"The story is tragic enough. I'm kind of glad that my dad didn't murder my mum. He sounds like a horrible man, though. This must be hard for you, as well. Raking all this up."

"Not a day goes by when I don't think about Kate. I curse bloody Jim, too. I'm glad to see that you have broken the curse."

"What do you mean?"

"I remember my mum being slapped by my dad. I was bullied by Jim, and by my first husband, if I'm honest. Kate was bullied and belittled by Hugh. You have a good husband. I had to be a lot older and wiser to work out what a decent man was. Thankfully, Jeff and I found each other and I've been happy ever since. You being adopted and seeing a better way of life, seems to have broken the chain."

Mike listened to Iris talk about meeting with her grandmother.

"A mixture of happiness and sadness then."

"Very much so. Tales of Kate falling off bikes and winning the sack race. Dancing with her friends and singing in her bedroom. Such ordinary things, but so poignant, now that she's gone. Poor Vicky, admitting that she's convinced her daughter killed herself. That was a horrible moment."

"She wasn't that keen on your dad."

"No. Having see the pictures and read the articles, I'm not surprised. He's not really the killer type. I think "feckless" is the best description of him. I'm not so anti him now. Just disappointed. My mum took up with someone who wasn't worthy of her."

"She had no real role models, I suppose. All her life she had only seen aggressive men. Hugh must have seemed like a better option."

"He wasn't violent, but he was still as unpleasant. He used words instead of his fists to control her. When he left, she would have realised what his true nature was. That would have been a contribution to her sense of despair. I keep trying to imagine what I would have done at nineteen with all of those burdens. I can't, because I had Tony and Sue. The two most reliable people in the world."

"And they are the reason that you didn't pick a wrong un and ended up with a lovely man like me."

"Indeed."

"An interesting comment about breaking the curse. It makes me hopeful, somehow. You've changed the dynamic of your family. Let's see if we can do the same for mine."

Chapter 45

Harold escorted Edith into the church. She was wearing a yellow dress and was carrying Bertie, who was in blue.

Doubtless, the baby would be handed to him, soon, because she would find it too tiring. The parade into the church for Henry and Mabel's wedding was a display for the rest of the Thomas family.

His son was quiet, but alert throughout the ceremony and his siblings clamoured to see and hold him afterwards. Edith found a seat and watched the proceedings from the side lines. Picking at her food like a sparrow, and sighing frequently, her reluctance to be at the celebration was obvious. Trying to engage her in conversation was hard work, but some tried.

"How lovely to see you, Edith. I hope you are well."

"A little tired. How are you?"

The exchanges only mentioned health, the weather, or Bertie. None of the comments were made with any enthusiasm. Harold could see that she wasn't well, but also that Edith didn't want to be there. It was time to remove her from the situation and head home.

As they said their goodbyes, Edith was wilting even more. They took a taxi cab to their home and she went to her bed as soon as she was through the door. The maid had been given the day off, so Harold cared for and fed Bertie. Finally, he settled the baby and he looked in on Edith.

"How are you feeling?"

"Just weary. I haven't been in a place with so many people for a long time. It was overwhelming. Is Bertie sleeping?"

"Yes. He should be good for a few hours. I think I'll go out and take a walk. Stretch my legs. Will you be alright on your own?"

"Yes. Don't be long, though."

Harold had his coat on and was out of the door before she could change her mind. He walked briskly to the bordello where he hoped to see Lottie. He had only been with her two days ago, but he had rather taken to her. It was a disappointment to find that she was not available, but he found what he needed elsewhere.

The next day, Edith was even paler than usual. There was a slight sheen to her skin, as well. It was probably due to the exertion of going to the wedding, Harold thought. The next day, she looked even worse. Each breath was a struggle. The doctor was sent for and he informed his wife's parents that she was sick.

The house was full again. Harold and Edith, her parents, the doctor, a nurse and the maid got in each other's way as they moved around the small house. Tension was high and tempers frayed as Edith's condition deteriorated. It was amazing to them all, that she managed to survive for a few more days. Every gasp sounded like it would be her last.

Too frail and too ill, she died in her sleep. The doctor announced her death and whilst no one was surprised, they were all bereft.

"Her time was limited because of the tuberculosis, but I fear some other infection might have contributed to her death." the doctor declared.

"Where could she have got that?" her father asked.

"There is no way to know, sir. Has she been out recently, Mr Thomas?"

"She went shopping for a new dress. We went to my brother, Henry's, wedding. I'm out at work every day, mixing with many people. An infection could have come from anywhere."

"Probably that wedding. She didn't want to go. I knew it would tire her out, but it seems it has killed her."

Mr Hills, Edith's father, had found his culprit. Despite no evidence, the Thomas family were cast as the guilty parties. Harold could argue with him, but it was pointless. Also, his wife's body was lying upstairs and it was not the time or place. The narrative quickly became fixed. Edith had caught flu at the wedding and had died as a result.

Harold couldn't risk losing the money which was still coming from Edith's family. They wanted to contribute to Bertie's welfare and he was not going to turn the funds away. The Thomas family were the villains and this meant that he would never see them again.

At first, the family were bemused at being ostracised from the funeral and having their offers of help with Bertie rejected. The flu story was spreading and the Thomas's were not happy that the blame had been placed on them. A couple of confrontations with Harold and then the split between the family was permanent.

Chapter 46

Iris and Mike looked at the pictures that had been given to them following the scan. As predicted by her, it was a boy.

"What made you think it was a boy? Is it because that is what you wanted, or because you had some sort of weird female intuition thing." Mike asked.

"I just started thinking of the baby as him and it felt right. I'm relieved that it is a boy. I would have looked a bit daft if it wasn't. I'll tell the boss tomorrow. Even he has been giving me a few funny looks and he doesn't notice much."

"You are definitely looking like a pregnant lady, which I like very, much, by the way."

The announcement about her being pregnant was met with a wry smile from her boss. Especially as Wendy had hammed it up as she pretended to be hearing about it for the first time. He even went out and bought doughnuts to celebrate the good news. Her parents, Mel, Vicky and even Judy, got calls telling them that they were having a boy. It was a good day.

Another bit of news came when Maggie called and arranged to meet Iris and Mike for lunch at the weekend. There might not be any new information from her, but it would be good to meet a member of the Thomas family who they didn't really know.

In preparation. Iris made a note, on a bit of paper about some of the deaths in the Thomas family. During the initial phone call, she had talked about having a list of who had died. If Maggie brought any paperwork with her, they could compare as had been suggested. Not everyone made the list. She had to pretend that it was a passing interest, not an obsession.

They met at a country pub and settled themselves around a table in the bar. Maggie had chosen the venue because she knew that she could bring her dog with her. Benji was a fat corgi who waddled to his spot under the table and didn't move until lunch had ended.

"I can see you are a Thomas, Mike. Dark hair and those blue eyes. We come in all shapes and sizes, but those bits are always there. Was your dad similar?" Maggie said

"He was. My mum was short and slightly plump. I got my shape and colouring form him. My sister, who died, would have been like my mum, I think."

"She was one of the victims of the curse?"

"Yes. Stung by a swarm of bees."

"How awful. The good news that you are having a baby brought us together, but the deaths are a shadow over everything."

"Did you find any notes that your mother had kept?" Iris enquired.

"Yes, hang on a second. Yes, here they are. She had tiny writing, so I hope your eyesight is good. There's a list of people who died and how they were killed. I looked through it when I found it and was amazed. So many freak accidents. Are you worried that something will happen to your baby, too?"

Maggie had come right to the point. There was little point in denying it and Iris and Mike found themselves telling her what had happened so far, from ghost to séance. She nodded as they spoke and her face was grim at the end.

"When you called, I wondered if that was part of the reason. The whole curse thing has been taboo, in the family. Nobody talks about it. I think your mum made a few enquiries before she died, didn't she, Mike?"

"Yes. She became interested when Becky died. I was only about twenty when she told me what she had discovered. I thought it was all a bit fanciful and put it to the back of my mind."

"My mother spoke to your mum. She told all of us not to say anything. She's gone now, time has passed and it should be talked about. If I can help in any way, let me know."

"Thank you, Maggie. We tried to be a bit subtle, after Mike's mum was blocked when she asked. We have contacted different people, as well. We need anything that can give us more insights into Harold. Knowing his reasons behind all of this will hopefully help us fight him."

"Have you got anything from other members of the family?"

"A distant cousin has said they have a box of papers. They are sending it to us. A way to get rid of something from the loft, probably. Who knows what's in it, but we've got to follow every lead." Mike added.

"I wish I had more proof. All I've got is gossip and rumour. Juliet, a member of Henry's side of the family, was convinced that there was a ghost that appeared to Thomas's. Looks like that part is true. She also thought it was Harold. She said that he had killed his wife and blamed it on his brother. I don't know whether that is accurate. Everyone else went with the, catching flu at the wedding story. Legends start with an inkling of truth and then get twisted."

"All we've got to do is sort out the real story. It happened over a hundred years ago, and as you say, things get twisted." Iris mused.

"Now. Let's talk about your family and Iris's baby and some good things."

Chapter 47

Mike heaved the box onto the table. They had expected a few papers in a small box, but a massive weighty parcel had arrived. He paused, pen knife in hand and then began cutting through the tape. Iris peered over his shoulder as he managed to get to the contents. No neat files or papers in rubber bands. It was chaos.

They stood in silence contemplating the box in front of them. Mike shrugged and began taking handfuls of paper out and stacking them on the table. Iris joined in and, once out of the container, the volume seemed to have doubled in size. When they thought they had finished, another box was revealed at the bottom of the main one.

"I'll put the kettle on." Iris said.

"I don't know where to start. I think I'll grab a load and begin sorting through. Hopefully, it will become obvious what piles we need and then we can put them onto the right one. Get the less important stuff to one side and then have a proper look through the other papers."

"I'm voting, now, for a miscellaneous pile. There are bound to be things where you look at them, shake your head and haven't a clue what to do with them. That will save time agonising about where they should go."

"Good point."

A batch was in front of Mike and he was reading the first sheet of paper.

"A bill. I'll put it here. Bank statement, new pile. Letter, that's more useful. A pile for those."

There were postcards and greetings cards. Bills and bank statements. Letters, official and personal. They hadn't even got to the second box yet. Who knew what information might be in the paperwork. There could be a bill for an item which was of interest, or a line in a letter that gave vital details. The only thing to do was to go through and read every item.

"Remind me, when we've done with this lot, to have a good sort out and get rid of any unnecessary paperwork. Going through this lot is torture." Iris sighed.

"At least we've got a working system now. Bills sorted by address and date. Bank statements by date. Personal letters, other correspondence. Then the miscellaneous. That seems to be a larger pile. We're over halfway through. It's all downhill from here. Once the sorting is done then the fun part begins."

"The fun part? Nice try, Mike, but you're not selling it to me. I've read a bit of this stuff as I've been sorting it, and it's dull. Maybe the letters will be better."

The last piece of paper was allocated to a pile and they smiled and high fived.

"The other box?" Iris asked.

"Yep. Got to do a proper job."

Mike reached in and retrieved it, finding that it was heavy. The tape was cut and the lid removed. Inside, in perfect order, were diaries. The first was dated 1897.

"The mother lode." Iris breathed.

The piles of, carefully, sorted paper were abandoned as they lifted the first of the diaries from the box. Mike opened the diary and found the name of the author. Mabel Tipton. The image of the robust Mabel, who had married Henry, Reginald's brother, came to Iris's mind.

"Mabel Thomas."

"Yes. This first diary is two years before she got married."

They reached out and clasped hands. Both were saying a silent prayer that there was something in the diaries which would help them with Harold. Sat next to each other, they began to read what Mabel had written.

"It feels wrong reading someone's diary. I know she's dead, but these were her personal thoughts. The words of a young woman. I'd hate to think someone would read diaries I'd kept."

"Did you write a diary?"

"No, but that's not the point."

The entries were about friends, her dog and dresses. Halfway through 1897, she met a young man called Henry Thomas. Hearts appeared at the edge of the page and her feelings poured onto the pages. The stern, thickset, woman in the picture was difficult to equate with the giddy girl being revealed.

They skimmed a lot of the content. The first kiss with Henry, his declaration of love and the death of her dog, were the most significant things that she recorded. There were some arguments with her two sisters and consternation about her wayward curly hair, but Mabel's life, in a, middle class home, was not high on drama.

1897 was finished and they moved onto the next year. Henry asked Mabel to marry him and she said yes. She admitted to her diary that she had been so anxious to say yes, that he had barely got the question out before she answered. Her older sister was consumed with jealousy and the younger one was thrilled. Her parents were delighted, but concerned with the expense it would involve.

The arrangements for the wedding, the guest list and the food, were described in minute detail. There was no mention of Harold specifically, only a note that Henry's family had all been invited. The next year, 1899, might reveal more. Mike and Iris opened the diary and the first entry informed them that this was the year that Mabel Tipton would become Mabel Thomas. A few, practice signatures in her new name followed. It made Iris smile. She had done the same.

"Have you noticed how anodyne it all is. Even when she is arguing with her sisters, it's polite." Mike observed.

"I know. I'm thinking that she might not be inclined to dish the dirt on Harold. I notice that there's a bit of a gap after the wedding. They were too busy bonking for her to update her diary, I bet. Turn the page. Let's see what she says next. No mention of sex, I'm sure."

"Oh, here we go. Comments on some of the wedding guests. Dorothy wore a hideous dress. Charles was such fun. Harold's wife is so pretty, but she is very frail. At last, we get something. Surely, we'll get more about them now."

Chapter 48

Iris quite liked going to work, most of the time. There was the occasional annoying customer or computer glitch, but

she knew her job and could breeze through her days.
Lately, everything was harder. The pregnancy meant that
she was more tired than usual and there were, other,
pressing, things, that occupied her mind.

The constant thought was about Harold and who would die
when he was no longer thwarted. The diaries needed to be
read to see what information could be gleaned from them.
There was the pile of other papers that had arrived in the
box. Also, Iris wanted to look back further into her own
family. Add onto this the need to see friends and family as
often as possible, who knew how long she had to live, and
there weren't enough hours in the day.

Each weekend that came, brought with it a flurry of
activity. Visit her parents, make more calls to Mike's
relatives, reading and research and then there was
housework and shopping. Mike did his share. He would
cook and clean and do jobs around the house. They were
both exhausted every night when they finally got to bed.

Mel and Ian had offered to help with the research, but Mike was worried that something would be missed. A word or a mention that would mean something to him and Iris, but be overlooked by their friends. How awful would they feel if they made an error, as well.

Mabel's lists and recipes and boring minutiae were still being trawled through. Edith's death had been noted. It had been "horrible" and "so sad". It was a few weeks later before there was any more mention of it.

"It, says here that none of the family were invited to Edith's funeral. They'd asked when it would be and got no reply. Mabel has no idea why Harold would exclude them and says Henry was upset." Mike said.

"Let me see." Iris took the diary and read some more. "There is more about Edith. They don't know exactly what she died of, but suspect it was consumption. They wonder how Harold is coping with the baby. Oh, it says that Henry wrote a letter offering both condolences and help, if it was required, but again, no answer."

"It sounds like they don't know that they had been blamed."

"I'll keep going and see if that comes up."

Mike made tea and Iris read the diary. She felt rather sorry for Mabel. There was bewilderment at Harold's lack of contact at his time of need. He had been distant from the family for some time, but surely, he would want their support in the circumstances. Then there was a change of tone.

"Ooh, Mabel's not happy. Says that they have been blamed for giving Edith the flu at their wedding. She states that they have "practically been accused of murder". Denies that anyone present was ill. Henry has decided that they will wash their hands of Harold."

Mike took the diary and then read the entry. He continued with the task as Iris sorted out dinner. All her good intentions about cooking proper meals had lapsed. With so much on the agenda, there wasn't time to do anything other than shove something in the oven or microwave.

The diaries were not updated so much for the next few years. The newly married Mabel must have been busy making her new life with Henry. There were monthly laments that she had not become pregnant yet and then, in 1905, everything changed.

"God, this is boring. Mabel is pregnant now, and every twinge is being described. Don't look at me like that. Each and every one of your twinges is important to me. Mabel, who had her baby over a hundred years ago, not so much. She seems happy though. I've gone through a few months and there is no mention of Harold. They have deleted him from their lives."

"They have cancelled Harold, to use the vernacular."

"Indeed. There is talk about Henry's brother, Reginald, and the sister Elizabeth. Everyone is having babies. Her sisters are talked about often, too. A big happy family helping each other and meeting up. Harold missed out on all of this. Why did he blame them? Keep reading and see if anything turns up, I suppose."

"It gets more mysterious rather than less. Mabel is sure that nobody at the wedding was ill. Edith had consumption and was never going to live for long. I don't understand why he jumped to that conclusion. I hope to God that Mabel has written something about it."

At the end of the weekend, the diligent reading had moved them onto 1917 and two more children had been born to Henry and Mabel. Reginald and his wife had four kids and Elizabeth had two.

The entries had been grim reading since the war started. A list of friends and family who had died or came home injured. Most of the Thomas family straddled the war years, with Henry's siblings being too old to serve and their offspring too young. Elizabeth's husband was conscripted and there was much worry about him.

Through all the years, the children's progress was recorded. Note was made of childhood illnesses and significant moments in their lives, such as first steps and lost teeth. Harold was never mentioned until news reached them that Bertie had died.

Mabel wrote that they knew that Harold's son had gone off to war. His death had been registered and they were saddened that he had died so young. There had been glimpses of him over the years, but none of them really knew Bertie. They mourned him as they would any member of the family, despite his estrangement. Once again, they tried to contact Harold, and once again, no reply was forthcoming. There was a comment that Harold himself was "not well", though no details of what ailed him.

Iris and Mike knew that two things were about to happen to the Thomas family. Harold was going to die, and then, children would begin to be killed in strange accidents. It would be interesting to see what Mabel said about these events in her diary.

Chapter 49

What sort of life was this. Harold worked all the hours he could and then still struggled to make ends meet. He had a son to bring up and a nursemaid to pay. The support from his in-laws had ceased following another almighty row about Edith's death.

There was no forgiveness from Edith's father. He needed an explanation for his daughter's death. It was Harold's fault for making her pregnant and then his family had finished her off by giving her the flu. The doctor had said that she had got some sort of infection and it had hastened her end and a narrative had been made to fit.

The constant accusations and haranguing had been too much to bear. Despite the money he received from his in-laws, and the love they had for their grandson, he could not tolerate their hatred for him. They had been banished from his house and life. He now lived in isolation. A self-imposed punishment for his wife's death.

No one actually knew how Edith had caught the illness which caused her demise, but Harold had an idea. It was not from the wedding, but that was proving to be a convenient story. He could avoid any guilt by letting someone else take the blame. He was a bad man, but he couldn't change.

Once a week, he had to limit his visits because of financial reasons, Harold went to the bordello. It was a type of punishment, too. The girl he had called on, so many times, was no longer there. Lottie had died around the same time that Edith had died. He missed her more than he missed his wife. Now, he went to the place where she had been, to see a girl that wasn't her and felt the pain before he had the pleasure.

There were other ways to cope with his miserable existence. He terrorised the junior clerks that he worked with and he drank himself to oblivion, most nights. Harold knew that he was a bad man, but he didn't care. His life was terrible, so why not make other people suffer, as well.

Bertie. Having his son was a blessing and a curse. He loved his boy and felt proud of him as he grew strong, but he resented the cost of his care. It was easier when he was young. The nursemaid cared for him and he was in bed early. The weekends involved more interaction with his son, but it was not complicated. Keep him fed, keep him clean, and pay him some attention. As he got older, it was harder.

Harold had a chatty son. Bertie would go through the numbers and the colours. He would list animals and flowers. The constant questions were the most annoying. The questions about his mother and grandparents were the worst. Since the boy had started school, he wondered why his family was not like the ones his friends had.

"My mama died. She had a sickness called consumption and she was taken when I was only a few months old. I have no other family. It's just me and papa."

This is what Bertie told everyone, but he didn't really believe it. A woman had stopped him and his nanny on the street, once, and said that she was his grandma. He was warned not to tell his father about the incident.

Harold would leave the house in the morning, still suffering from the effects of drinking the night before. Bertie would recoil if he went near to him. The smell of alcohol on his breath made the child wrinkle his nose and, sometimes, wretch. Harold decided not to go near him anymore.

As Bertie grew up and understood more, the gulf between father and son got wider. They lived in the same house, but had little interaction. They butted heads on a regular basis. Information was being teased out of his father bit by bit.

"You, said that I have no other family, yet you now mention my uncle. Why don't I know any of my relatives?

"It was at a family wedding that your mother caught the flu, which killed her. Your grandparents blamed them and we cut them out of our lives."

"What about my grandparents? Why don't I see them?"

"They are horrible people. Blaming you and me for their daughter's death. Every time they came to the house, they would cause arguments. I'm surprised you don't remember all the rows. You were very young, but it must have been traumatic."

As time went by, and Bertie got older, he knew that the stories he had been told, were not true.

Chapter 50

Iris was back on the website, this time looking for her side of the family. She knew more about Kate and Vicky and, as she had the wherewithal to do so, wanted to go back further. The next person that she found was her great grandmother, Clara.

There were details of the men in the family, of course, but Iris was drawn to the females. Their stories were, so far, rather tragic. Her own mother dead at nineteen, her grandmother bullied and abused, and now the life of Clara was being revealed. This was turning out to be a humdinger.

Vicky had given some of the information and Iris was now reading about it in a newspaper article from the time. Poor Clara was married to a bigamist. Her husband, William, was prosecuted and got a, measly, six months in prison.

"I was only about nine or ten when it all kicked off. My dad, William, had been married before he met my mum. She was told that he was divorced and never questioned it. Then, a woman turned up on the doorstep looking for him and the story came out. He was still, legally married to her." Vicky had said.

The story in the paper made a great deal about how Clara was actually an unmarried mother to two children, Vicky and her brother Simon. There was more drama about that, than the fact that William had committed bigamy. The stigma of the situation, back in the sixties, was very different to the present day, when no one really cared.

Clara stood by her man and waited for him to get a divorce and then marry her properly.

"I think she did it for me and Simon. It meant that we were legitimate, not a couple of bastards. Heard that name applied to me a lot when it all happened. It didn't last though. He had lied to her and she never got over it. Four years later, they decided to divorce. Then she got cancer and died.

As if that wasn't bad enough, he, my dad, then goes back to his first wife, taking us kids with him. We had an older half-brother, John, and my step mum got landed with all of us. I think he only went back to her, so that she would look after us. I wouldn't mind, but he was nothing special. I don't know why either woman put up with him.

She was alright, though, my step-mother, considering we were dumped on her. I didn't have a lot of time for my dad, but I liked her. I visited her until she died, a couple of years ago. John and his family send Christmas cards, but I haven't seen him for a long time."

With each tale of tragedy, Iris was more determined to not be another of Harold's victim. It was the twenty-first century and time for women to be allowed to live out their lives without suffering at the hands of men. Harold would be fought against to her last breath.

Mike was reading the newspaper clipping about Clara. Shaking his head, he put it down and sighed.

"Bloody hell, Iris. The women in your family have had a really rough time. Like you say, it's almost as if they are cursed, too. Are you going to look back further?"

"A little bit. I'm hoping to find someone who has led a, fairly, ordinary life. I need to know that some of my ancestors were happy."

The story of Clara filled Iris's thoughts. Every day she appreciated Mike more. They had come close to losing each other, but the whole thing with Harold, had brought them back together. It would be heart breaking if their happiness was cut short by him. Whether it was her, or their child, that died, it would have a terrible effect on their lives.

Iris stroked her stomach. It was an unconscious action which she did often. It was spending time with the son who she might only know for a short time. The clock was ticking and they had to work out how to thwart Harold, permanently. The reading of the diaries and the calls to members of the Thomas family continued, but it was hard to maintain enthusiasm, despite what was at stake. If only they could get some good news.

They took any positives they could find. Everything with the pregnancy was progressing smoothly. Iris had only suffered morning sickness for a short time and, so far, apart form fatigue, it was not proving to be a problem. Mike, the financial manager for an engineering company for the last fifteen years, was being invited to join the board. A proper stake in the business he looked after with such care.

If they could get through this ordeal, what a life they could have. Iris thought about them, with their son, maybe another child, too, holidaying abroad. They could buy a bigger house. Yes, one with a big kitchen diner, like in the magazines. There was no way Harold could be allowed to win and take all of that away.

Chapter 51

The diary in front of Iris was dated 1918. This was about to

get interesting. Harold was dying and it wouldn't be long

before he started his vendetta against the Thomas family.

What would Mabel record about these events. Scanning the

first few months, she then came across what she had been

looking for. Harold's death.

It was noted that the "poor man" had died at the age of

forty-two. Mabel said that he had no life and had been

bitter and twisted since the death of Edith. When he lost

Bertie, his decline had been rapid. The problem was

alcohol. He had drunk far too much for far too long and his

body could take no more.

The family, despite being rejected for so many years,

attended the funeral. Mabel and Henry were embarrassed to

be recipients of Harold's assets. He had left no will, but along with Reginald and Elizabeth, they were his next of kin. They had never wanted his money, only his friendship. He had some meagre savings, a few decorative objects and some furniture. It was divided up, with the, most sought after items, being Edith's jewellery.

The ruby ring was mentioned, because it had gone to Reginald's wife. As the eldest brother's spouse, she had been given first choice of the jewels and she had picked it out straight away. Mabel and Elizabeth had both had their eyes on it and were disappointed when it was snapped up.

More lists and recipes followed. The occasional social engagements were noted, mainly family gatherings, and then came the awful news of young Henry's death.

"You okay, love?" Mike asked.

Iris reached for a tissue and mopped at her eyes.

"Henry has just been killed by the horse. Mabel is devastated. She say's she can't stop crying and is afraid to let her other children out of her sight. Henry said he saw a swirl of smoke before the horse bolted and wondered if it was a firecracker. Whatever it was, it had spooked the horse and that had resulted in their son's death."

"Sadly, I think we know what it was."

"The first, or one of the first, sightings of Harold's ghost. At this point it was just a freak accident. I wonder how many more occurred before the family began thinking of it as a curse."

"I would say, one, an accident, two, unlucky, three, a curse."

"Who is next? Elizabeth's daughter Abigail, I think. Not until 1920. I wonder what Mabel says about that? I'll keep reading this one, even though it's tempting to jump ahead."

It was many months before Mabel didn't mention Henry in every diary entry. Iris imagined that one never got over losing a child and prayed that she would never know that pain. Another year went by without any major incident and then it was onto 1920.

"I'm turning the pages, dreading what I'm going to find. I don't think I can keep reading it right now."

"Here, hand it over. I'll look at the rest of it."

"It's the anticipation. I know that Abigail is going to die and I can't bear waiting for it to happen. Poor Mabel will be all upset again. I'm so sorry now that I commented on her sour face. Wherever you are Mabel, please forgive me and I feel your pain."

Mike took on the grim task of scouring Mabel's diary for 1920. He had not gone far when the death of Abigail was recorded. First Henry, now Abigail. The sentence was repeated over and over by Mabel. There appeared to be some confusion about what had killed the young girl. It was a few weeks before the link with the poisonous mushrooms was made.

An interesting note was made about Abigail loving to play in the garden on her own. She would chat away to herself and inspect the various plants and insects.

"Probably chatting to Harold." Mike said after telling Iris about this development.

It would be a year until the next death. Mabel mentioned Henry and Abigail occasionally. She always grouped them together as if their deaths were linked, but she could not have known it at the time. Some sort of instinct perhaps. Mabel and Elizabeth had been friends for years, but their bond deepened after the loss of their children. They mourned together and were frequent visitors to each other's houses. They found comfort in being with someone who understood what they were going through.

There were allusions to something else in the diaries. Secrets between the women which could not be committed to paper. It was tantalising and infuriating. Mabel would talk about "the Harold thing" or "the Abigail thing". Mike and Iris could guess all they wanted, but they might never know what these "things" were.

Chapter 52

Mel was visiting and getting an update on the research. The diaries were arranged in the box and she gazed at them before picking one out for closer perusal. Absorbed for a few minutes, she looked up and rolled her eyes.

"Good God, how are you reading these things without becoming brain dead. If I see another sentence about how sweet her dog is, I might give up the will to live. Oh, poor choice of words there. Sorry."

"I'm glad you're here Mel. It has been hard work reading these things and I need a bit of a break. Yes, there's all the boring stuff, but then, sadly, the weird deaths are recorded in them, too. I'm starting on 1921 now, and I know another one is coming. This will be the third. One from each of the families of Harold's siblings. Mike thinks that after the third, the legend of the curse will become a thing."

"Three deaths from three families. Each of them a bizarre accident. All within a couple of years?"

"Yes. 1918, 1920 and 1921."

"It would be amazing if suspicions weren't aroused. What was the reaction from Mabel to the first two?"

"Well, the first one, Henry was her son."

"Oh no. I'd forgotten that. Heartbroken, I presume."

"Yes. Months of mourning. Just when she is coming to terms with it, you never get over it, Abigail, Elizabeth's daughter dies. More mourning and a bonding between Mabel and Elizabeth after the loss of their children. There is something going on, though, that is only alluded to. I think that the women were putting it together before Lucille dies. There are cryptic references to the "Harold thing", like he was involved."

"They don't say anything else. How frustrating. You have to read all of the rest of the diaries in the hope that it will all become clear, I suppose."

"Yes. Wading through the recipes, lists, boring details and annoying snippets of something just out of reach. Change of subject. How's Ian?"

"He is wonderful. He does, irritating things, every now and then, but I don't mind. I think the stars had to align, or something, before I could learn to give and take. The look on your face tells me that you recognised this fault before I did. I know, you couldn't tell me, I had to find out for myself. Better late than never, eh."

"You've found the right man. Things fall into place when that happens. I felt so comfortable with Mike from the beginning. There was a rough patch, I told you about that, but everything is back in perspective. I know, for sure, that Mike was, and always will be, the one for me."

As with every visit now, Mel and Iris shared a few hugs and a few tears. Although Mel offered to stay whilst Iris read about Lucille's death, she was sent on her way. 1921 had to be tackled and it was time to get it over and done with.

The news of Lucille's death was reported with the words "another one".

Mabel noted that the poor child had been hanged by a ribbon around her neck getting caught on a door handle. A cruel accident, she said. Then, another of those observations that made the hair stand up on Iris's arms. "Elizabeth and I agree that we cannot distress Elspeth further with our notions about Harold at this time."

"Mike. Come and look at this."

He appeared in the kitchen doorway, newspaper in hand and a worried look. He took the diary from his wife and read the paragraph she was pointing to.

"Bloody hell."

A comment had been written, but no further explanation. Discussions must have been going on between Elizabeth and Mabel that involved Harold and the deaths. Surely, there would be more about this in the following diaries.

The family attended another funeral of a child. Mabel hoped that she would not be wearing black again for a long time. Iris thought that, with one child from each of the sibling's families dead, they probably hoped that Harold had sated his need for vengeance. The next generation, however, would suffer, as well.

Iris looked at the picture of Mabel. Thickset and sour faced, she stared defiantly at the observer. She was amazed that Harold had the nerve to cross this formidable woman. There must be a way to channel her strength in this fight. Returning to the original box, Iris found Mabel's death certificate. She had died in 1951, having lived through two world wars and the ravages of the curse.

What a woman. Iris admired Mabel for so many reasons. Her love of family. The support she had given Elizabeth. The intelligence to put the clues about Harold together. Yes, there was a lot of dross to read through, but the answer to the riddles had to be in the diaries somewhere. Please don't leave me without an answer, Iris begged.

Chapter 53

Harold still had his job. That was the only positive thing he could say about his life. As a chief clerk, he told people what to do, rather than did it himself. This was fortunate, because his struggles with alcohol were making it more difficult to function by the day. At some point, he would be found out and then all would be lost.

Bertie and him lived in the same house, but rarely communicated. Harold's drunkenness made it hard to have a conversation or a relationship. It was often down to the maid to pass messages between the two men. Some news, however, needed to be delivered face to face.

"I've joined the army."

"You've done what?"

Harold emerged through the fog of alcohol to register what his son had just said.

"I've joined the army. I passed the medical and have taken the vow. I head off to training camp in a couple of days."

"What on earth possessed you to do that?"

"It's my duty."

"You stupid young fool. You are going to your death."

"If that is what happens, so be it. I can't stand back whilst others my age are going to war."

"I have brought you up on my own. Paid for everything you need. You repay me by throwing your life away in this war."

"You didn't bring me up, a nurse and then maids did. Sorry to have been such a drain on your resources. Think of the money you will save when you don't have to feed and clothe me anymore."

These weren't quite the last words that they spoke to each other, but there was not much of an improvement in the tone. A goodbye and a handshake were grudgingly given before Bertie left for his training. There was a brief visit before leaving for the front, during which both men remained mostly silent. A pat on the back from Harold sent Bertie on his way.

Harold could not be considered an optimist. He went to work, came home, drank and waited for a telegram to arrive. Each day dragged by and he anticipated the relief that a notice would bring. Better to know for sure that his son had died rather than spend each day in a state of anxiety. It was a strange logic, but his whole life was, somehow upside down.

Each day, the turmoil in his stomach became worse. His eyes, they weren't good either. Of an evening he would blackout, losing several hours, before staggering into his office where he had, lately, been caught napping on a few occasions. Harold knew alcohol was dangerous. He knew it could shorten his life. He knew he could lose his job. He didn't care.

The drink was damaging, but necessary. Harold could not look back on his past without regret. He saw no future because he could not get over the past. Oblivion was his only refuge. The wait went on. Neighbours, colleagues and strangers were receiving the sad news of another soldier killed in this dreadful war. No one had come to his door.

Harold had wished it and now it came true. Bertie had been away for five months when the knock on the door came. He felt calm as he opened the missive and saw exactly what he had been expecting. The reaction was to open a bottle of gin and have a drink. The black out came shortly after that first swig.

The next morning, with an almost superhuman effort, Harold made it to his place of work. The worried glances were now shocked stares. Pale and shaking he trudged through the office to his room. It was not long before the

owner of the business arrived and looked at him with

disgust.

"Good Lord, Harold. What is wrong with you?"

"My son…"

"What about your son?"

"Dead."

"Oh. I see. Perhaps you should take the day off. I'll get a

cab to take you home."

The return walk through the office, saw the clerks and

other workers averting their eyes. Harold shuffled along as

if he were one hundred years old. Tempted to offer his arm,

the owner hovered slowly beside him, hands poised to

catch him should he fall. A collective sigh of relief could

be heard when he exited the door.

Once back at home, Harold took to his bed. Within reach, were a number of bottles and a cup. Should he wake and think about Bertie, he had the wherewithal to become unconscious and forget again. He would never return to work.

Chapter 54

Reading the diaries was hard work. Much of what was contained within, was boring, but Iris was beginning to feel an affinity with Mabel. There were occasional flashes of a keen sense of humour, describing a neighbour as looking like chimney sweep's brush. A little sketch in the diary showed a, thin women with wild hair.

"Henry says that I am illogical. The only logical conclusion to that, is that he is wrong." Mabel wrote. Iris couldn't imagine Henry disagreeing with his wife that often. She doubted that he would come out best. She could only do the diaries in short bursts. Time for a change of task.

Iris had resumed her search for members of her family. She was now looking at the details of Clara's mother. Jane Miller, nee Hills, had married a banker, Daniel. Their early life was comfortable and happy, but, at the relatively young age of forty-six, Daniel suffered a stroke. He never made a full recovery and was left with difficulties speaking and walking until he died twenty years later.

Jane nursed her husband through the years. Iris got a sense that they were in love and she tended to him without resentment. Not quite the happy story that Iris had been looking for, but Jane had married a good man and she stuck by him until the end. There was a daughter, Clara, and two sons, George and Christopher.

Clara had died of cancer, but Jane was taken in by her eldest son George when Daniel died. There was little money by this time, with Daniel unable to work for so long, and she relied on the charity of her family.

Jane would have been alive at the same time as Harold. Her address showed that they had not lived far from each other. Iris wondered if they had ever crossed paths. It took a while to find a photograph of Jane. It revealed an attractive woman, small and slim, like all of the women in Iris's family, who was beautifully dressed. She would have swept past Harold in a swirl of silk, as he walked, head down and, likely, mumbling under his breath.

Mike saw the smile on his wife's face and stroked her shoulders as he walked by. He put the kettle on and then came back and gently rubbed her stomach.

"You look happier. Not on the diaries of gloom today?"

"No. I'm giving myself a break. It's been a tough journey, but I think I've found a happy ancestor. Jane Miller.

Happily married, three children. Lived with her eldest son George when her husband died. Here's a picture of her."

"Quite a beauty. Now I know where you got it from."

"You are saying all the right things. Now, if you top that off with making me tea, I'll be the happiest wife ever."

Mike delivered the tea and took the laptop from Iris to read all about her ancestor, Jane. Iris watched his face as he began to read. She liked looking at him as he was lost in concentration. The frown on his face was a little unexpected and then he got up and left the room.

A moment later, Mike returned, clutching the photo album from his mothers box. He opened it and then pulled one of the pictures out. The photograph of Edith was put next to the one of Jane.

"Edith's maiden name was Hills. Jane's maiden name was Hills. Look at the pictures. Do you think they were related in some way?"

Iris would have sat bolt upright, but her bump made that tricky. She did scrabble to lean over and inspect the pictures more closely. Picking them up, an examination was carried out and she nodded.

"Could be. A few searches on the website and I should be able to find out."

Iris sat back after furious tapping on the keyboard and reading and making notes.

"Okay, hold onto your hat. Edith and Jane were cousins. Their fathers were brothers. I'm saying this out loud, and as I'm talking, I'm staggered by the coincidences here. Our families linked so long ago. There's something in this Mike. A symmetry. A closing of a circle. I don't know how this will work, but I'm sure it will be to our advantage."

"Good God. I think we both need to take this all in."

"There is every likelihood that my great, great, grandmother, Jane met your great, great, uncle Harold.

Even if they weren't close, I would have thought Jane would have been at Edith's funeral. I wonder what she thought of him. Did she get to see Bertie and maybe hold him for a while?"

"If we ever get Harold at a séance again, there is a lot that we need to ask him. Before we banish him and put an end to the curse, of course."

"I'm going to find out all I can about the women in my family. I want to know more about Jane and Clara. I want to find out about my mother Kate. I've been toying with trying to contact my father and I think that I need to do it. This is about me. That sounds a bit egocentric, but you know what I mean. Mine, or my baby's, life is being threatened. I should have all the information I can about my clan. I don't know why it's important, but it is."

"I've thought about your father, too. I understand why you need to meet him. He could be a nice bloke or a massive tool, but that is not the point. It's learning what he is and then, if necessary, leaving him behind and moving on."

"Exactly that. I hope he can tell me about my mum. Her frame of mind before he left. What their relationship was like. I know it's a cliché, but I also want to know if he ever thought about me. I will be disappointed if he says no, but I will get over it and move on."

"I suspect that you have already found out where he is. Phone call, or doorstep?"

"Definitely doorstep. I think Hugh might be a bit of a slippery one."

Chapter 55

"I hope he's there. All this travelling, to then find he's out or doesn't live there anymore, would be beyond frustrating."

"I'm on edge, Iris, so I can't imagine how you must be feeling. About five minutes, now and we will find out."

"I wonder what he'll think when he sees a pregnant woman on his doorstep. He'll probably be desperately trying to remember if I'm someone he's dated and impregnated."

"You've got him marked down as a rogue, then. I must admit he looks a bit suave in his pictures."

"I think he will act like he did when he was thirty. Still thinks he's got it and that women adore him."

"Well, we are about to find out. Range Rover in the drive. Looks like he's home."

Their footsteps crunched across the gravel as they made their way to the door. A glance at each other, for courage, and then Iris pressed the bell. A few seconds later, her father, Hugh, appeared and his first reaction was to turn white and stagger back in horror.

"Are you alright?"

Mike caught his arm, to stop him falling, and Hugh managed to look away from Iris to the man beside her.

"Yes, yes. I thought you were someone else. Gave me a bit of a shock."

"Did you think I was Kate?"

"Oh, God. You're the daughter." Hugh's legs nearly gave way again.

They all shuffled inside, helping the poor man to a seat in the lounge. Hugh waved his hand towards a drinks trolley and Mike poured him a brandy.

"Sorry about that. I never intended to cause you distress. I'm Iris and I wanted to meet you, but didn't want to give you the opportunity to say no. A bit forward, I know, but you are my father. I will understand if you don't want to have any sort of relationship with me, I'm not sure that I want that myself, but I needed to meet you."

After a few gulps of brandy, and with the colour returning to his cheeks, Hugh found his voice.

"That was certainly a shock. You look just like her. With you being pregnant as well, it was like you were a ghost from the past. I think we need tea. It will give me a moment to get my head around this. Let's adjourn to the kitchen."

They left the comfortable lounge and Iris found herself in the kind of kitchen she had longed for. An island in the middle, marble work surfaces and even a wine fridge. Hugh used loose tea and a teapot and Iris wasn't surprised.

"Okay. I'm going to address the thorny subject first. Your mother's death. I was out of the picture when it happened.

We were at the point where we knew our relationship was not going to work. She told me to leave and I did. Did she really want me to go, or was it a gamble to make me stay? I've thought about that a lot since. Only in the last, say, ten years, have I had the courage to accept my role in what occurred. I didn't kill her, but I'm still partly to blame."

"I met Kate's mother, my grandmother, Vicky, and she thought that it was suicide. She has regrets, too. She couldn't help Kate more because of her partner at the time. Hindsight is not often a good thing. Anyway, I was curious about you and, of course, eager to hear any stories about Kate. That was what brought me and Mike here."

"Well, your timing is impeccable. In the past, if I'm honest, I was a shiftless sort of fellow. Always looking for the easy way. Relying on my family. Lost a lot of what I had, so I suppose I learned the hard way. If you had met me back then, I'd have run for the hills. I'm still in shock, you understand, but I'm not afraid or appalled."

"I'm glad about that." Iris smiled.

The tension had eased and, as a prelude to more conversation, they wandered around the garden, with their cups of tea. Back inside they resumed. He was in the mood to talk, perhaps he was always like that, so Iris let him tell his story.

"Kate was pretty, so, ergo, you are pretty, too. Can't see much of me in you, which is probably for the best. I didn't think I was the type to settle down, but I gave it a try. I got married and had two sons, but messed that up by playing away from home. Stupid thing to do. Anyway, I still see the boys, your half-brothers I suppose.

"Kate. She was wise. You know, one of those people that is young, but has a lot more common sense than everyone else her age. Her home life wasn't good and we kind of collided. I gave her a place to live and she gave me the companionship I needed. I think we both knew it could only be temporary. Then the pregnancy confused everything.

She was clever. Not in an academic way. She didn't take Latin at school, as I had done. Not that it has ever done me much good. She learned things, asked questions, wanted to be better. I don't think she would have hurt herself if she had been in her right mind. She was practical and inventive. There would have been a way for her to cope with having a kid. I think that she had post-natal depression. An accumulation of troubles, from me leaving, to the situation with her mother, made it all too much."

"I appreciate you being honest with me Hugh. I didn't think about my real parents for years. The people who adopted me are wonderful and I never felt the need. When I became pregnant, it seemed more important."

"I often wondered if you would turn up one day. Dreaded it for a long while and now I'm quite pleased. Good God, this means that I'm going to be a grandfather. Grandpapa Hugh. I'll have to tell the boys. They're called Timothy, after my father, and Louis. Fine lads, if I say so myself. Their mother is a lot more responsible than me and has to take all the credit."

Mike and Iris left having made promises to keep in touch. They were not sure it would happen.

Chapter 56

Kate knew that her relationship with Hugh would end, when she found out she was pregnant. He was handsome and a lot of fun. Racing around town in his open top car. Eating at the finest restaurants. She had tried so many new types of food since she had met him. Indian cuisine was her favourite because of the spices.

At nineteen, she was young, slim and pretty. His eyes had

followed her across the room on the first night they met.

Kate met his gaze. She was in the pub with a couple of

friends and she moved away from them, ditching her half

of lager on a table. Screeching girl with beer, was not the

impression she wanted to create. A few minutes later,

sipping a glass of white wine, she learned his name was

Hugh.

Her mum, Vicky, was a good woman, but she had a terrible

choice in men. Her father had been vicious with his words,

putting his wife down and criticising her every action. This

new bloke, Jim, was not so subtle. He used his fists. There

was no way she could convince her mother to leave him,

not once she had Carl, so, not wanting to see the daily

battles, Kate had moved in with Hugh a few weeks after

they had met.

The first few months that they were together, were

wonderful. Parties, clothes and lots of sex. Kate thought

that she was in love. As the gloss wore off, as she knew it would, it was not replaced with a calmer more comfortable life. What came next was a gradual realisation that Hugh was fairly useless at everything apart from parties and sex.

News of her pregnancy was met with horror. Hugh's face told her what he really felt. Attempts to seem pleased were not convincing. Of course, she would have to tell her mother, too.

The tears in Vicky's eyes, when she heard the news, were hurtful, but not unexpected.

"A baby is a wonderful thing, Kate, but it will be hard for you. What does Hugh say about it?"

"He's fine."

"I haven't got much, but if you need anything."

They were saying the right things, but none of it was real. Hugh wasn't fine. Vicky couldn't help her.

Kate watched Hugh struggle with the situation. He thought of himself as a gentleman and, as much as he wanted to escape, duty kept him around. It was obvious and heart breaking, but the only solution was to let him go. When he arrived home one evening, she was packed and ready to go.

"Looks like you're going. I don't get any say in this then."

"Be honest with yourself, Hugh. You don't want a family. You don't want to settle down. You want fun and laughter and parties."

"That's what you think."

"That's what I know."

"Where are you going. Not back to your mum's."

"I've got somewhere."

"Well, you best be off then. Here, a tenner, then you can get a taxi to wherever you're going. Let me know when my child is born. I'll give you some money to help."

Picking up the carrier bags full of clothes, Kate managed to get out of the place before she cried. It was the only thing to do, but it still hurt. Hugh had looked sad. Some part of him cared about her.

The baby was born. A girl. Kate loved her, but felt so inadequate. One minute, she was wearing designer clothes and swanning around at country houses and now she was a single mother in a hostel. Her mother had visited and offered her a fiver. Poor woman. It was all she could smuggle out of the house without Jim noticing.

What sort of life would her baby, as yet unnamed, have. What sort of life would she have. No money, no family to help, no chance that she could live like the wealthy people she had rubbed shoulders with. Hugh was gone. He'd left his apartment and disappeared. She was utterly alone.

The baby girl was handed to a friend at the hospital. She was going out to clear her head, she said. The friend didn't mind. She had seen Kate struggle to bond with the child. Reluctant to pick her up and she had not even been given a name. Hours later, when she hadn't returned, the alarm was raised. Kate's tragic end was almost inevitable.

Chapter 57

"A game of two halves, I think they say. Hugh was exactly what I thought he would be when he was younger. He's changed in the last few years, just in time for us to meet him. I was, fairly sure that I wouldn't want anything to do with him, but I'm prepared to think again." Iris said.

"You must want to meet your brothers, too."

"Yes, I do. What we didn't establish was whether he had told his ex and the boys that he had another child."

"That could be a very interesting conversation. Grandpapa Hugh. That made me laugh. I will insist that our child never uses that name."

"He was a bit of a toff, wasn't he. Did you see the outdoor swimming pool? I could see myself sat next to that with a gin and tonic on a summer's afternoon. Grandpapa Hugh with the baby on his lap and you playing cricket, or some such thing, with Timothy and Louis."

They were laughing now.

"Seriously, what are your expectations. Do you think Hugh will be a regular part of our lives?" Mike asked.

"I'm not sure. I would like to keep in touch, but realise that he might have other commitments. Even if it was just Christmas cards, I would be happy. Anything else is a bonus."

"I'm glad he wasn't a rotter."

"A cad."

Mike and Iris were in high spirits. The meeting had gone much better than they expected. It was good to laugh again. They eyed the diaries and declared that they could wait another day. Iris called Mel and invited her and Ian over for an impromptu get together. They could catch up with all that had happened. There was a lot to talk about.

"Okay my brain hurts. Your great, great, grandmother was related to Edith, Harold's wife." Mel massaged her temples as she spoke.

"Yes. I don't know why, but I think that finding out all about it will help us."

"How?"

"That's what I've got to work out."

"And we met Hugh." Mike added.

"Iris. I leave you alone for a couple of days and then find out that you have been off all over the place having adventures. What was Hugh like."

"Who's Hugh?" Ian was confused.

"Hugh is my dad, who I've never met before. I didn't know anything about him until a few weeks ago. Mel and I had looked him up on the internet. I wasn't sure about meeting him. In the end, I needed to find out what he was like, so we drove to his place this morning."

"We thought that he looked like a bit of a scoundrel. You know, a lady's man, and a dodgy dealer." Mel explained.

"And was he?" Ian wanted to know.

"An ex-scoundrel I would say. We nearly killed him before we had a chance to talk. He looked at me, pregnant, and so like my mother, and thought he was seeing a ghost. I hadn't even thought about it, but I can see why he was so shocked. He was honest about his shortcomings and talked about his guilt for leaving my mum."

"He also said that he would not have welcomed us a few years ago, but he has become more self-aware. He messed up his marriage and I think it had a sobering effect on him. He realised that he is going to be a grandfather and referred to himself as grandpapa Hugh." Mike said.

The photographs were out again. Kate, Vicky, Clara and Jane were very similar. Iris looked like them, too. It was as if, whoever the father was, the female genes were dominant. Seeing her family with their light brown hair, Iris had already decided to forgo the highlights. She wanted to be like them. Edith was added to the group, as well. Although pale and tiny, she had the same features as the rest of them.

"I'm finding a lot of strong women in both our families. Jane caring for her sick husband. Clara divorcing her bigamist husband. Vicky getting rid of her bullying partner and finding a good man. And don't start me on Mabel Thomas. That woman was a rock."

"Girl power." Mel said.

They raised their glasses to the women.

"Talking of strong ladies, have you spoken to Judy lately?" Mel asked.

"No. That is something that I must do. I want to tell her about the link between Jane and Edith. I'm sure she'll find it fascinating. Maybe even helpful in some way. If we have to call Harold back again, the fact that I'm related to his wife, might make him stop. Mike and I have talked about it and think it is something that could sway him. If he's doing all this to avenge his wife, why would he inflict pain on her family."

"That is a good angle. The question is, can Harold be reasoned with. Nothing he has done for the last hundred years has been rational. Have you found anything in the diaries yet that could help?" Ian said.

"No, but we've got years to go yet. Some more ammunition would be good. Like you say, Harold probably won't be swayed, but if we could hit him with a number of reasons why he should stop, it could work."

Everyone looked at Mike after what he had said, but none of them seemed hopeful. The mood was beginning to dip until someone mentioned grandpapa Hugh again and the smiles were back.

Chapter 58

Judy and Iris spoke briefly, and then decided that a face-to-face conversation would be better.

"I haven't seen your bump yet, so, yes, I would love to visit. It sounds like you have a lot to tell me."

Hugging, as Judy walked through the door, they felt like old friends despite having only met on one momentous occasion. Harold, swirling around, smashing crockery, was imprinted on their memories.

Iris had prepared for the meeting by doing her own, very basic, family tree. It showed the line from Jane to herself and the link between her great, great, grandmother and Edith. Judy heard the stories of the women and was astounded about the link to Harold.

"We thought that if we told Harold that I'm related to Edith, it might make him back off. It would be a conflict, I suppose. His need for vengeance against the Thomas family, versus protecting a member of Edith's family. The question is, would it make any difference, or is he just hell bent on revenge."

"At some point we are going to have to call him back again. I don't know that we can have a rational conversation with him, but we can try."

"Any progress on the idea to banish him."

"It's not really gaining traction in the community. I wish I had something better to tell you, but I can understand the reluctance. It's not been done before and Harold is a dangerous spirit. I still think that there might be something in having numbers on our side. A few more people to attend the next séance. It could make an impression if there were a few people telling him to stop."

"I'll work on a list of people I think will be receptive to the idea. We've already recruited Mel's other half, Ian. He says that he was visited by his grandmother's spirit on the night she died, so he wants to help ay way he can. Shame there isn't a ghost trap, like in those films, that would make life easier."

"God, yes. I call them up, someone presses a button, and they're gone. That would be brilliant."

"Meanwhile, back in the real world, we're still grinding our way through Mabel's diaries. She knew, or seemed to know, after the second death in the family, that Harold was involved. I don't know how, she hasn't revealed that, but I'm hoping that it will all be become clear at some point.

"It was difficult for people in that era. Certain subjects were taboo, and they wouldn't even commit them to paper." Judy said

"I get the idea that she is afraid to write down her thoughts and suspicions. So, time passing could make her more inclined to give details. The world is a bit more modern. People are a bit more tolerant. Also, more deaths happen and that must solidify what she already half believes."

"I hope so. How much longer before the baby comes?"

"Another three months."

"Ideally, we should have the séance sooner rather than later. We know that you are safe whilst you are pregnant. Who knows how soon after the birth Harold might strike. Of course, it could be years before he makes his move, but you don't want that hanging over you."

"You're right."

"Have you thought what you are going to name your son yet?"

"At the moment, we've got as far as, anything but Harold. Luckily, I'm having a straightforward pregnancy, because we just don't have time for other things like hospital appointments. The other thing that's eating away at me, is that there are some people I haven't told, about Harold. My parents. My new family. Do I prepare them for tragedy, or let it unfold."

"Two things. They will be devastated if you die suddenly, or if they know you are going to die. Secondly, if we can find a solution, you won't die. Well, not at Harold's hands, anyway. Thirdly, I know I said two things, but I've just thought of another, I would love to hear about the new family members you have met."

They spent an hour talking all things family. Iris's adoptive parents, Vicky and Carl and her dad Hugh. She had shown Judy the family tree, but now she talked more about their lives and their troubles.

Judy spoke about her, now deceased, husband. No, she had never tried to contact him. Her son was a police officer, and no, he didn't ask her to call up murder victims. They were happy to let each other do their thing. If he asked at any point, she would be glad to try to help with one of his cases, though.

Mike stuck his head around the door occasionally and, each time, the women were deep in conversation. In the end, he went in the kitchen and took a seat at the table. He was soon involved in discussions. When Judy left, they sat in silence for a while.

"She's right. We need to decide on a strategy and call Harold back." Mike said.

"I'm nearly there. Let's read the rest of the diaries, then we'll have a summit and plan what we are going to do. There is something. I can't put it into words. A feeling, I suppose, that an answer is within reach. I lay awake at night, but I can't force it. It will come, I'm sure."

Chapter 59

The diaries were attacked with renewed vigour. Judy's visit had prompted Mike and Iris to get the job done. The reading was a bit easier for a while. The children of Harold's siblings had not yet grown up and had children of their own. There were no more deaths for a while. That, of course, would change.

Mabel was getting older, but still had her fire. Waspish observations of the people around her continued, "Mrs Formby wears the colour grey, a lot and it matches her disposition.". There was nothing about Harold for many years. She must have thought that his actions were finished.

A sad point was when Henry died. He had been ill for a few months before he went. Mabel, mourned him, but also reflected on their life together. It had been a good marriage. The loss of young Henry was the only major trauma during the years. The war brought more privations and losses, Then, in 1945, peace was declared.

The celebrations for VE Day brought the family together. Mabel, with the aid of a walking stick, joined the revellers in the town centre. Singing, dancing and fireworks made it a joyous day. A few months later a new tragedy changed everything.

Mabel wrote about the awful accident that had taken Mary, her granddaughter's life. The child had fallen from a train. There were smudges on the page from Mabel's tears that she had shed when writing. It was time, she said, to talk about what had been happening.

Iris tapped mike on the arm and pointed to the diary. Words came eventually.

"Mabel says she is going to talk about the Harold thing. Here we go"

"For many years, I have held certain things secret. I did not even talk to my dear husband about them. Elizabeth has been my confidant, because she is part of this story. It begins with my son Henry. His death, shortly after the death of Henry's brother Harold, was devastating. When Abigail died, the family could hardly bear the loss.

Elizabeth and I talked often and a surprising detail emerged.

"Abigail loved the garden. She inspected all the flowers and the insects. Elizabeth would watch her chat to herself as she skipped around. Then, her illness came. In her delirium, Abigail talked about her friend. He showed her the mushrooms. The name of her friend, who nobody had ever seen, she said, was Harold.

"Elizabeth was confused and scared. After Abigail died, lost in her grief, she did not focus on Harold, or the mushrooms. When the cause of death was discussed, she remembered the words and was chilled.

"We discussed the death of Harold's wife and the ridiculous story of her catching flu at the wedding. His bitterness towards the family and his estrangement had affected all our lives. Was he now, after his death, carrying out some sort of vendetta towards the Thomas's? The death of poor Lucille, seemed to put it beyond doubt.

"The strangeness of the deaths was a red flag. Such horrors seemed to be designed to cause the maximum pain to us. A child from each of his siblings' families. A cruel revenge for the death of Edith. Now, it has started again. Mary, from the next generation has died. The accident followed by a wisp of smoke. A tell-tale sign of his interference.

"All of this misery has been perpetrated by Harold. I can only think that he has come to believe his own lie, that the Thomas family caused Edith's demise. I know it was a lie. I have not said anything prior to this, to protect Harold's reputation, but, no longer."

Iris paused and her and Mike exchanged a glance. They held hands as she read the next part.

"I saw Harold visiting a brothel. It was near a hat shop that I frequented. I asked the staff about the place and was told a most interesting story. The gentleman that had just gone in, they said, was often there. He had been particularly attached to one of the girls, who had died of influenza. I asked them when that was and the date revealed was a few days before Edith had died. He had visited a prostitute and picked up an illness that he passed on to his wife. He killed Edith."

"Fuck"

Mike looked shocked. Partly at the story and partly at Iris swearing. Something she rarely did.

"The lying bastard. He knew that the Thomas's weren't responsible, but he took it out on them because he couldn't face the truth. He killed Edith. Not directly, not deliberately, but it was his actions that led to her catching flu. How dare he take my sister and my parents. How dare he threaten you and our child."

Mike's hands were shaking. Iris nodded and her mouth set in a hard line.

"We need to put an end to Harold.

Chapter 60

Harold lay in his bed. He was used to having a hangover. In reality, he had a perpetual hangover. They way he was feeling now was a whole new level of pain. He was not going to seek help for his troubles. This was what he deserved.

Trapped in his bed, he could barely move his body, there were just his thoughts to occupy him. A rolling parade of the mistakes he had made. Not acknowledging that the beautiful Edith was frail and ill before they married. Going along with the Hill's family assertion that the flu had been caught at Henry and Mabel's wedding and, therefore, blaming his family for his wife's death. Cutting them out of his life.

Then, there was Bertie. An inquisitive bright child, who he couldn't find time for. The boy who posed many questions that he wasn't prepared to answer. The drink. That had been his way to cope, but it had also taken him away from his child. The boy became a man and became a stranger.

His son had gone off to war and had not come back. There was nothing at home for him, so his decision was regrettable, but understandable. Harold had almost wished death upon him. The telegram had brought an end to the anxiety of not knowing, but had replaced it with the terrible sense of loss. An accumulation that had resulted in his present circumstances Bed bound and dying.

The maid came and cleaned him up and brought him food. She also delivered his bottles of gin. He had to pay her more than usual for undertaking the ghastly jobs. It didn't matter about the money. Harold's mind was in turmoil, but he realised that he would not live much longer. He would drink his gin and think his dismal thoughts until he died.

What a pathetic man he was. Pushed around and conned by the Hills family. Avoiding and blaming his family rather than face the truth. Finally, he admitted to himself, the facts about Edith's death. He had visited Lottie and she had been ill. He had thought he loved the prostitute, but her sickness had not prevented him from taking what he wanted. His selfish actions had led to him carrying the infection back to his own household.

The maid had gone home. He howled his rage to the empty house. No. He would not take the blame. Believe that it was the wedding. Believe that the Thomas's killed Edith. It wasn't his fault. Mr Hills was right. That damned wedding.

What would happen when he faced Edith? The gaze full of sadness and recriminations would be hard to look upon. He didn't want to see her again. There must be an effort to evade her judgment.

"I'll stay. In some form, I'll stay. They must believe, like I do, that they are to blame. The Thomas's will know and they will pay. Yes, Retribution."

Raving into the night, he had made his mind up. As his body failed, his determination grew. When his corpse went to the grave his will would cling onto the real world. He had things to do. Havoc to wreak. People to torment. A grim, determined, smile was on his face as he drew his last breath.

The next morning, the, long suffering, maid found Harold dead. She would have to notify someone. She would have to find a new job. He had no family. None that he spoke to, anyway. The house was searched and she took a few things of value. There was some cash. He had cufflinks and a fob watch. She looked at Edith's jewellery, but didn't touch it because it was tainted, somehow.

When the door was closed as the maid went to the doctor's office, she left Harold in his own filth. Her job was done. She would not do another service for the miserable old man who she had served for years. There was not an ounce of regret for her decision.

Chapter 61

Iris opened the box that Mike's mother had left for him. In the corner was the container with the ring. She took it out and studied it. Questions formed in her mind. Why did the ring keep coming back? Would Harold take the time out from his deadly endeavours to retrieve a ring? Why hadn't she thought about this before?

The thought of trying the jewel on, had seemed wrong, but now the urge to do so was overwhelming. It slid onto the ring finger of her right hand and felt as if it had always been there. Another question. If Harold hadn't brought it back, who had? The only candidate she could think of was Edith.

Frail in life, was she also weak in the afterlife? Iris thought that she would not be able to stop Harold, but a message of some sort was being sent. What was it? For the next few days, she wore the ring. An idea was forming.

The message, Iris decided, was, don't give up. Edith was there watching what was happening. Unable to do anything herself, she needed those who were alive to help in some way. The epiphany came in the middle of the night. When she got up in the morning, her Saturday started with a cup of strong tea and a pad and pen. Time to get organised.

The night had brought wild dreams and nightmares. The faces of the Thomas family and her own ancestors paraded through her mind. Mabel, fierce stare and a tiny hat. Edith, pale and so thin that a strong gust of wind would have toppled her. Elizabeth, with a haunted look following the death of her daughter. The victims of Harold's hate were there, too. Abigail and Lucille. Children who had died before their lives had really started, leaving behind shattered parents.

Her own family appeared. The photographs of them, had showed smiling faces. Petite women who were hiding their personal tragedies. Jane, watching the husband she adored suffer a stroke. Clara, cheated and lied to before succumbing to cancer. And her mother Kate. Her circumstances and despair had led to her taking her own life.

Harold kept cropping up, as well. There was no stopping him butting in and trying to ruin everything. In her dream, the formidable ladies from the past, formed a barrier to try to protect her and her baby from him.

The spirits from beyond were helping her. In the land of the living, she had support, too. The wonderful parents who had adopted her, Sue and Tony. Her best friend, Mel, now joined by Ian, they would do anything for her. New family had come into her life. The timing for that was fortuitous. Vicky and her partner, Jeff, would step up, if required. Maggie, Mike's relative, she was involved in all of this, as well.

This was more than a dream. It was a plan. The next morning Iris made lists of names. A guest list for a séance.

"Morning. You look, energised?"

"I am Mike. I have a plan."

"A Harold type plan?"

"Oh, yes."

"Come on, what is this plan?"

"I think that Edith's ring kept coming back because she was returning it, not Harold. She knows what has been happening, but can't stop him. She needs our help. Our strength. Judy said something about getting more people to a séance. We need to be ganging up on Harold. Mel mentioned girl power. I'm putting all these things together. I need to recruit some help."

"Who are you going to recruit?"

"My parents. Vicky and Jeff and Maggie. We will have Mel and Ian. That's the living people. We'll also call up Edith, Mabel and Elizabeth. The girls that died, Abigail, Lucille and Mary. I want Jane, Clara and my mum, Kate, there, too."

"We've got all these people. What happens next?"

"We make Harold face the facts. He gave his wife the flu and I am related to Edith. The women who have been wronged, those who have stood strong, they will act, together with the good men, you Ian and Jeff, to confront him and make him confess his part and move on."

Mike thought about all of this for a minute. Iris waited in silence.

"Okay. What do we need to do?"

"We need to visit people. We need to tell them the story of Harold and the curse. We need them to believe enough to come to the séance. Maggie, she'll do it, I'm sure. She already knows about the curse and the pain that goes with it. She will want to help. I'll call her and see when she is free. My parents will do whatever I ask them, but I want then to understand and be as committed as they can be to it. My mum will be fine. My dad is the one who will need persuading."

"I'll come with you when you speak to them. He sees me as sensible, and if I'm on board, it will help him accept it."

"Yes, good. I know I've only met Vicky a couple of times, but I think this being about a put upon woman and a bullying man, will convince her to join in."

"Also, Harold is threatening you and her grandchild. Yes, she'll be up for it."

"We'll have to speak to Judy, of course. She is the one who will have to call all of these people."

"Can she do that?"

"Yes. I'm certain she can. I think these people are waiting to be called. They will want to help."

"The last question is, where are we going to hold this séance, because they won't all fit in our kitchen."

Chapter 62

Mike was not quite as enthusiastic about Iris's plan, but it was the best idea they had. He had noticed that his wife was wearing Edith's ring and asked her about it.

"You've got the ruby ring on."

"Yes. I felt like I should wear it. You're looking at me like I'm mad, but I needed to try it. I think it will help."

Help with what? Mike didn't ask for clarification, but it had given her an enthusiasm and, most importantly, hope.

The plan, once revealed, had a crazy kind of logic. All of the women wronged by Harold, gathered together, would be a formidable force. Edith, killed, indirectly, by his philandering. The mothers whose children had been killed simply because they were part of the Thomas family. Iris's ancestors who had all been bullied or abandoned by the men in their lives.

Men had a more positive role in the grand séance. They were a representation of good men. The antithesis of Harold and the lousy husbands and partners. They wouldn't be there to keep the women in line, or tell them what to do. They were there to support and empower the women.

The person that Iris hadn't mentioned was his mother. She had lost a child, too. Maybe she thought that he wouldn't want her called back to face Harold. Mike didn't question his wife about it. The list of people to be called had been specific. Those attending the séance were carefully chosen. This was her idea and he would let her do what she felt was right.

Iris had not had any problems with her pregnancy. She had been a bit tired at times, but nothing more. Mike was worried about what the forthcoming events might do to her. If Harold turned up and started flinging things around again, she could be hurt or go into labour. She was seven months gone and that was too soon for this baby to come out.

At work, Mike made some notes. A pros and cons of the séance. The first thing to recognise, was that Iris was determined to do it. So, what might happen. Someone could die. Harold had done it many times before and he would not hesitate to do it again. Maybe he wouldn't wait for the birth of their baby. He might just get the job done and take Iris.

It could be someone else. It could be him. How would they feel if their séance killed one of their friends or family? A shudder, before he shook it off and continued with his list. Judy would call all these people and no one would turn up. Only Harold would turn up. They somehow managed to make him stronger, unlikely, but worth considering.

Thoughts of his mother and father and Becky filled his mind. The box of information had been left to him for a reason. Mabel's diaries had found their way to them. The ring that Iris was wearing. Coincidences or some divine plan? He couldn't quite make the leap, but Iris had tuned into everyone, somehow. She had taken all the threads and knitted them together. To her, there was a logic which brought her to her conclusion.

Judy had said that she could do what was asked of her. They needed to tell others the story of the curse and persuade them to attend the séance, but that felt like a formality. Those on the list would be there. Nothing would stop them.

The noting down of the pros and cons was abandoned. There were a number of problems and the only good thing would be if their plan worked. Worrying about it wouldn't change the outcome. Mike had to go with the flow. He wasn't sure that he would enjoy being part of this enterprise, but he could go into it with the same enthusiasm as Iris.

Iris believed the séance would work. He believed in Iris. Mel and Ian, who had been with them all the way, would be there and would be resolute in their support. Sue and Tony would fight for their adopted daughter. Vicky and Jeff would be doing it for the unborn great grandchild. Maggie was a Thomas and this was personal.

All they needed now was a venue and a date. This event was now an unstoppable force. Mike hoped that Harold wasn't an immovable object. Then he remembered that they had Mabel on their side and it all seemed a lot more positive.

Chapter 63

They had found out what they needed from Mabel's diaries, but Iris wanted to read them all. She finished 1945 and picked up the next one. At the beginning of 1946,

Mabel began to refer to the deaths in the family as "the curse". It preoccupied her thoughts and she seemed determined to make as many notes about it as she could.

There was a whole section devoted to reports of the children having seen a ghost. Dredging back in her memory, she recalled her own son talking about his friend who stopped him falling into the canal. Henry didn't know the name of this hero, and hadn't really seen him, he had just felt a shove that changed his momentum from forward into the water to backward, away from it.

Mary had sworn that she had a guardian angel. On the day that she fell from the train, the family had seen a wisp of smoke slither out of the open door. Her own husband had mentioned some smoke when the horse had bolted towards her son, as well. More stories emerged as she dug into the rumours, just as Mike's mum had done all those years later. The mist had even appeared at one of the deaths in Australia.

The deceased were listed, together with the cause of death. What strange reading it was seeing the inventive ways Harold had killed people. Iris thought she should update it with all the ones that had happened after Mabel's death.

The writing was getting untidy as Mabel grew older. It seems that she had tried talking to her children about the curse, but they were reluctant to believe, what they thought, were the wild stories of an old woman who was becoming senile. Desperate to keep her archive safe, she made the family promise to keep her diaries and pass them down through the generations. She was sure that someone would need them some day.

How right you were Mabel, and thank you, Iris thought. The last diary was filled with peoples' names. Family, friends and neighbours. It was as if writing their details down preserved their memory.

There were just Christian names, full names and, next to some of them, descriptions or anecdotes. Iris would never know any of them and yet she smiled, and sometimes cried, when she read about them. There were poignant tributes to those she had loved. Her son and husband, Abigail and Lucille, her sisters and parents.

There was no farewell. No indication that she knew her time was up. The last entry was about having some delicious cake. Iris thought that this was a fitting finale to the story. Not maudlin or tragic. No dramatic deathbed confession or laying down a curse of her own. A slice of cake and then she died.

The diary for 1950 was put alongside the others and Iris put the lid back onto the box. At that moment, she made a promise to Mabel to keep the diaries and pass them onto her son. She would get some sort of fancy box or glass case to put them in. Something more fitting than the cardboard box they currently inhabited.

"I think we both became rather fond of Mabel. Despite the trivia and the horrible recipes." Mike said.

"Yes. I liked her. I don't think I'll be boiling any beef or mutton any time soon though."

"That's what you meant when you said they were waiting. Mabel left this legacy to help with Harold at some point in the future."

"I think so. She'll make sure that Elizabeth and the others are there, too. I'll think of her every time I eat cake now. In fact, after this child, we must have a daughter so that she can have Mabel as a middle name.

"What about all the other strong women? The other Thomas's and the ones on your side? We'll either have to have a lot of daughters, or one with about ten middle names."

Iris couldn't say it out loud yet, but they were looking to the future. The chances of thwarting Harold had gone up considerably in the last couple of days. They had a plan. Meetings were arranged and her and Mike would now go out and use all their persuasive powers to get everyone to the séance. She better run it all past Judy, too.

Chapter 64

Judy listened to the plan and, after clarifying a few points, was enthusiastic about it.

"Like you say, your kitchen is going to be a bit small. I have an idea about a venue. Let me make some calls and I'll get back to you. I should be nervous about doing it, but I'm excited. I can almost feel the energy and we haven't even got everyone together yet."

Maggie didn't need any persuasion. She was eager to confront Harold and play her part in putting a stop to his murder spree.

"Too right I'm going to be there. Just let me know when and I'll be ready to help in any way I can. It's about time that someone challenged that man, or ghost, or whatever he is."

"Of course, we'll come to your séance, darling. Just tell us when it is."

"Hang on a moment, Sue. I need to understand all of this. Mike, you said you had seen this ghost, Harold."

"Yes, Tony. Not so much of a ghost, as a swirl of mist, but things were thrown around and we heard his voice. I know this all sounds crazy, but we have a lot of evidence. The diaries that we talked about. The records of the strange deaths. Iris's friend Mel had seen him, before the séance, and Iris herself has seen him a number of times."

"This ghost has hurt people in the past and has threatened Iris."

"Yes. That's why it's so important that we do everything we can to stop him. He has killed about a dozen members of the Thomas family. He killed my sister and my parents."

"How does he do it? How does he make these things happen?"

"I don't know the mechanics, Tony. We might ask, why is he still here after death. Where was he supposed to go? Is there a heaven and a hell? People have had freak accidents which have caused their deaths. The common denominator is Harold. This is where we have to take a leap of faith and go with it."

Iris nodded and grasped Mike's hand. He had expressed it perfectly. Tony sighed and then glanced at Sue.

"Looks like we're going to a séance."

A group hug was the only response. Having got them on board, iris now delivered the trickier news.

"We need a lot of people there to accomplish what we want. I'm asking people that have my best interests at heart and are connected to both my and Mike's families. Mel and her boyfriend Ian will be there. Mike's relative Maggie. I'm also asking my grandmother, Vicky and her partner Jeff to attend."

A pause turned into a minute as Tony and Sue absorbed the information.

"She has lost her daughter, she will want to help you." Tony said.

Hugging again.

On the walk home, Mike tackled another thorny issue.

"You told them about all the people that are going, but you didn't mention the ghosts."

"I think that was enough for today. I'll talk to them about that another time."

"Right. Off to Vicky's then?"

"Yes. I liked the leap of faith bit, by the way. Dad must have been thrown by that. You're the logic and numbers man and then you are asking him to trust when there is no proof."

"He got it, though. Some things don't have a neat answer. He took the leap."

Vicky and Jeff listened to the story. She was angry.

"This Harold. He can't be allowed to hurt anyone else. We've got to do this Jeff."

"Yes, indeed. I want to be there. What a fascinating project to take part in. You say a séance. What does this entail?"

"A medium, Judy, will be there. She will talk to everyone taking part before we begin. A number of people will attend. My parents, my best friend, one of Mike's relatives and you two."

"And Harold, I suppose. He will be the one you are calling?" Jeff asked.

"Yes. We have a plan. We need to put a few more things in place and then we will give you a time and place. I'm so grateful for your help with this. It means a lot to me."

It had been a busy day and Mike and Iris were glad to be home. They had talked in the car about the plans so far.

"No mention of the ghosts again."

"I know. The things is, Mike, one of the people I want to be there is their daughter. I thought Vicky would be anxious, at the very least, if she knew that it was a possibility. I think we will have to get everyone there and then use the emotion that is unleashed."

Chapter 65

Tony and Sue sat at their kitchen table for several minutes after Mike and Iris left. Sue stood and went and filled the kettle, as if in a trance. Mugs of tea were in front of them both and, after a sip, they were able to break the spell and discuss what had just happened.

"I want to check that I've understood what is going on." Sue spoke first.

"Okay."

"Iris is being followed by a ghost and this means that she, or her baby, are going to die."

"The ghost is Harold, one of Mike's ancestors."

"Yes, and he has killed lots of people. Children."

"That seems to be the long and short of it. Iris thinks that the séance will help her get rid of him, with our help. If I hadn't heard it from Mike, who is usually so sensible, I wouldn't even be entertaining the idea."

"I know you are struggling to accept this, Tony, but it's for Iris. If she wants something, we must help."

"Of course. It's all a bit overwhelming and worrying. So much has changed in the last few months. Iris is pregnant, then she's asking about her biological parents. Next thing, we learn that she's met her grandmother Vicky. My head is spinning."

"I know that's been hard. I worried about what she might find and if she would be rejected again. Then I worried that she would swan off with her new found family and forget about us. All of that was stupid. Iris loves us and we love her."

"I had all those thoughts, too. I came to the same conclusion as you. Iris is ours and always will be. We just have to share her a bit. How do you feel about meeting Vicky?"

"Oh, Lord. That is tough. Knowing a bit about her life and the decisions she made has helped. The way she has accepted Iris and wants to build a relationship is good. An open mind on this one, I think. What about you?"

"Sue, if you and Iris are happy then so am I. When I say happy, I mean okay."

"The only thing I know about seances, is how they are depicted on television. I'm still a bit surprised that they are a real thing."

"I'm going to look it up on the computer. Like Mike, I need to have a few facts and figures to help me take it all in. Make us another cuppa, Sue and I'll see what there is about seances on the internet. A load of old nonsense, probably, but it's worth a go."

The next mug was deposited under his nose as he peered at the screen through his reading glasses. Sue had never seen her husband so thoroughly distracted from his garden.

"Things will never be the same again." Sue declared.

"What do you mean?"

"We've been plodding along in our rut. I'm not complaining, but we have become a bit set in our ways. Before long, we are going to have a grandchild. We will be babysitting and going to the zoo. We will have to learn about all the fashions and fads, all the new music, as he grows up. We need to, what is it they say, get with the programme."

"Good lord. Here we go again. You're not going to start listening to rap music, are you? I don't think I could cope with that whether the boy likes it or not."

"Oh, they will have some new type of thing by the time he's at school and taking notice of that stuff."

"I hope so."

Tony sighed.

"This is what it's all about, isn't it. Saving Iris and her son. Mike talked about a leap of faith and you've reminded me of what's at stake. Now, let me get back to the research and stay in my rut for just a little longer."

"I wonder what I should wear to the séance?"

Tony raised his eyebrows and Sue went off to look through her wardrobe.

Chapter 66

"Okay, I've got a place for the séance." Judy announced.

"Brilliant, where is it?" Iris squeaked rather than spoke.

"Five miles outside town, is an old barn. It's empty apart from a few hay bales. No old farming equipment with sharp metal edges. We don't want to tempt Harold. I've sent a couple of pictures, and the directions, to you, so you can have a look."

"Yes, got them. It looks perfect, Judy. It's not too big, so we won't look lost in it. Arrange the bales, sit in a circle and do your thing. I think we ought to allow time before we start for some chat. We need to introduce the participants to each other and I expect you will want to talk to them about what will happen."

"If we meet about 7pm, then we can get around to doing the séance about 7.30 or 8."

"Right, and the date?"

"Friday?"

"Great. I'll round everyone up and make sure they are all headed there at the correct time."

"All set then." Mike said.

For the first time since making the plan, Iris had a wobble. The theory, such that it was, and planning, had kept her occupied, but now she had to hope that they pulled it off. The look on her face told Mike how she was feeling.

"Don't doubt yourself now, Iris. You know the people who are going to be with us, the ones we are going to call and why they are necessary. Judy has found a great venue and is ready and eager to do this. We will pull this off, I know it."

"Pre match nerves. I'll be alright once we're there and it all gets going. We've got so much invested in this. It's got to work."

Calls were made to everyone. Maggie was fine with the date. Her parents were a yes and would travel with them. Mel and Ian could barely wait until the date. Vicky and Jeff had been waiting for the go and were ready.

The next two days at work were almost unbearable. Wendy watched Iris with worry.

"Are you okay? You seem on edge. You even glared at a customer today."

"Oh, yes. A bit hormonal, I think. I get a little tired, now. I can't wait for my maternity leave to start."

"I'll speak to the boss and see if you can go early, today."

"Hold fire. I'd rather get out early on Friday, if I can. I've got things to do."

"No problem. I'll get it sorted."

"Thanks, Wendy."

The day had arrived. Her mother had phoned to ask what Iris was wearing. Not aware of any specific séance etiquette, she told Sue to wear something comfortable. Her and Mike picked them up at 6.30pm and they were off to the barn.

They were the first to arrive, with Judy following a couple

of minutes later. Mel and Ian, Maggie and Vicky and Jeff

were soon in the barn, too. Iris made the introductions and

she was pleased to see that her mum and Vicky were soon

deep in conversation. Maggie joined them and the three

older women looked comfortable in each other's company.

It was twilight. A couple of lamps were the only

illumination they had inside the barn. It was gloomy and

chilly, which was fitting for the occasion. The men were

dragging the hay bales into a tight circle. They needed to

be able to join hands. Tiny Judy climbed on top of one of

the bales to make her speech to the friends and family of

Mike and Iris.

"Thank you all for coming. You know that we are going to

hold a séance, the purpose of which is to banish the spirit

of Harold Thomas from the plane he currently resides in.

He has hurt people and is now threatening Iris and her

baby, so our task here, today, is of vital importance.

"Iris and Mike have unearthed evidence of the truth about his wife, Edith's death, which we will put to him when he is called. Ideally, faced with the facts, he will give up his quest for vengeance. Sadly, reason will not likely apply to this situation, so we have a back-up plan.

"We will call upon our ancestors to return and help us remove him. Edith, Mabel, Elizabeth, Abigail and Lucille, from Mike's family. Jane, Clara and Kate, from Iris's family. These are all women who have shown great strength, or suffered at the hands of men. A spectral army of females who will, no doubt, overwhelm Harold and make him leave.

"What can we expect. When Harold was called before, he threw things around and shouted and wailed. A ghostly tantrum, one could say. I think it might get a bit loud in here, with everyone's voices. Don't panic. I can dismiss them all, if necessary, but I would like to let things play out for as long as possible.

"I can see Vicky and Iris, who I know would love to talk to Clara and Kate, but we have to deal with Harold first, and then, if they are inclined, the spirits might spend some time with us. I can make no promises, though.

"I need you all to focus. Project your power. Okay. Is everyone ready? Let's do this."

Chapter 67

Total silence. Not a breeze or bird song. Nature was holding its breath at the same time as those assembled in the barn. They were sat on the hay bales, holding hands and Judy had her eyes closed, concentrating on her task.

Everyone felt a vibration. Glances were exchanged. Any doubt about whether contact had been made was dispelled when a voiced boomed out.

"WHAT?"

"Hello Harold. I'll tell you what. We are here to put an end to your murderous actions. Your campaign of revenge must stop. Why? Because the Thomas family were not responsible for the death of Edith. You were. Also, Iris, who you have threatened, is a relative of your beloved wife." Judy was not messing around.

"NO"

"Yes, Harold. We know about your visits to the brothel. We know about Lottie and her sad death."

The walls of the barn rattled, as two large branches crashed through the doors and flew across the room. Everyone ducked. A couple of people screamed. Judy stood up. The tiny woman faced the mist that swirled close to Iris.

"The truth doesn't matter to you then. Plan B."

Closing her eyes and throwing up her hands, Judy shouted her command.

"Come on ladies. We need you now. Edith, Mabel and Elizabeth. Those who died at your hands, Abigail, Lucille and Mary. Edith's and Iris's family, Jane, Clara and Kate. Join us now and help us get rid of Harold and his curse."

A burst of light announced the arrival of the women. The intense beam dispersed and bathed the interior of the barn with a soft amber glow. The mist that was Harold, moved into the circle of hay bales. It swept around close to the people. It was a threat.

The light shimmered and became ten beams, which flashed across the barn and encircled Harold. The grey smoke became denser and a shape began to form. They could all clearly see that it was a man. They watched as his mouth opened and he howled with rage.

"Go on, girls, Get him." Iris screamed.

The others joined in, shouting their encouragement. Mel jumped up and down as she yelled and Vicky, Sue and Maggie held hands as they shrieked. Judy was back on the hay bale punching the air as the attack on Harold started. The men weren't bystanders. They roared their approval and cheered as the light spun around the Harold shaped mist and this time, his spirit did not voice his defiance, his cry was one of agony.

The bales moved and the hay, getting free from the string, was caught up in the melee, which was now a tornado in the middle of the barn. Wisps of grey smoke snaked out of the column of light and hay, but were quickly dragged back in. The voices of the female spirits gave the order.

"GO."

The light intensified, making everyone shield their eyes, and then an incandescent flash. Everything was still. Stalks of hay drifted back to the ground and the barn was dark after the bright light. The cacophony of a few seconds earlier had gone and they waited.

Judy stepped down from the broken bale and then held up a hand. Focus switched to her.

"Mabel is here."

They all edged closed to Judy and saw a soft glow next to her.

"She is representing the spirits that we called today. Harold is gone. You and your baby are safe, Iris. They were all elated to get the chance to remove Harold and they thank us for giving them the chance. Clara and Kate saw you Vicky and they saw Iris. They are glad that you reunited. They are at peace.

"We called nine women, but there were ten who came. Your mother was here, too, Mike. She wanted to see the work that she did, come to fruition. She is happy now, too."

They all cried. Relief, elation, the messages from beyond, each had their own reason for doing so. After the tears came the joy. An awful lot of hugging and kissing was going on. Judy was a bit flabbergasted at what she had done. The praise and thanks of the group were bonuses. Iris gave the closing speech.

"Judy, thank you for orchestrating, what has to be, the greatest séance of all time. Harold came when you called. The women came, too. You got them in the same place at the same time.

"Thank you to all of you who believed and lent us your focus and energy. It was pretty scary there for a while, but then it was magnificent. I think, in the end, we are all glad that we were here and proud of what we've done. Our voices joined with the spirits and we told Harold to go to hell."

Chapter 68

They were all too excited to head home. Everyone wanted
to talk about what had happened and their personal
thoughts and experiences.

"When you threw your arms up to the sky and yelled
"Come on Ladies", that was amazing." Iris said.

"A touch theatrical, I confess, but it felt right. You
screaming "get him girls" a moment later, really got things
going. The room was electric. I looked around at
everybody cheering and shouting and I knew, at that point,
we couldn't fail. The spirits of the women, our energy,
Harold couldn't fight against all of that. I saw you with
your phone, Ian. Did you capture any of it on video. I could
travel the world giving talks if you have" Judy replied.

"I pressed the buttons and pointed the camera, but nothing seems to have recorded. Well, not pictures anyway. The sound is there. Let me play it."

Harold's wailing, the shouting, the rustling of the hay in it's whirlwind and the ghostly sound of the women telling him to go, could be heard. A chorus of people asked for a copy and Ian started pressing buttons on his phone.

"I didn't even think about the number of women called and the beams of light. My mum was here, joining in. Of course, she would want to come. She did her investigations. Harold took her daughter. It's fitting that she was a part of it. It means that she also saw Iris and knows that her grandchild is on the way."

Mike spoke with tears streaming down his cheeks. Soon, everyone was dabbing at their eyes.

"A message from my mum and daughter. The fact that they came back to help Iris. This has been the greatest day." Vicky said, still dazed by the experience.

"It was terrifying, thrilling and glorious. I'm so glad I was here. Sorry to anyone I partially deafened with my screams. I got a bit carried away." Mel said

"Sorry I doubted you, Chicken. Your mum and I are so glad that we came. I still can't quite believe what we saw. The most important thing, is that Harold has been defeated and you and your baby are safe. It was amazing, but I hope that I don't ever have to go to another séance in my life." Tony declared.

"I'll second that." Sue added.

"I'm so proud of the Thomas women. We knew Mabel was formidable, so Harold was in danger. Add Iris's relatives and he didn't stand a chance. It was done for all of the children and people he killed. It was done to save Iris.

There was energy and determination, but there was also so much love in this room." Maggie summed it up.

People readied themselves to leave. Maggie said that she had to get back to Benji, her dog and everybody else, at the very least, needed a cuppa and a chance to unwind. A convoy of cars drove back along the lane which led to the barn.

Iris was weary when they got home. The tension of the day began to seep away and she slumped into a chair.

"I don't think we can put it off any longer. We need to think of a name for our son." Mike said as he put a mug of cocoa in front of her.

"All those ancestors. I don't know whether to choose one of those names, or go for something new."

"There have already been a lot called Henry. I quite like the, old fashioned names rather than something modern or made up. What haven't we seen in the records?"

"Edward. I don't remember seeing an Edward. I like that. Maybe Henry as a middle name, as it seems to be a bit of a tradition."

"Edward Henry Thomas. Eddie Thomas, a bit gangster. Ed Thomas. Yes Ed, he could do anything he set his mind to."

"I've thought about names a lot, but I've been afraid to say anything out loud. Now we can look forward to meeting Edward, rather than dread what might happen after he's born. I still can't believe we did it, Mike. Those beams of light. They were a perfect representation of their spirits."

"Yes, Light beating the dark. Mabel. It was right that she was the one to talk at the end. Her diaries led us to the truth."

"Your mum would have got there, too, if she'd had more time. We made that call and got the box. That changed everything."

"Luck and timing. Maybe fate. Whatever the reason, we got the necessary elements together and got rid of Harold. We saved you and generations to come. I think you ought to add an addendum to Mabel's diaries. Explain what we did and how it all turned out fine."

"That's a nice idea. As soon as I go on maternity leave, which can't come soon enough, I'll start on it."

Chapter 69

Edward Henry Thomas, weighed in at 8lb 1oz. He had his father's piercing blue eyes and Iris's light brown hair. The birth was fairly straightforward, the boy was cute and the parents, after a few days of panic, settled into a routine and were very happy.

The few frantic weeks before the baby was born, had left them exhausted. Mike and Iris didn't miss the furious activity and planning that they had been forced to undertake. They were fully embracing the quiet life. Well, quiet when Edward wasn't demanding something from them.

Mel had nagged so much, that Iris couldn't say no to making her Edward's godmother. She had always been the preferred choice. Those who had attended the séance would be lifelong friends. They would be at the naming ceremony for the latest addition to the Thomas family and would, no doubt, be around at birthdays for years to come.

Vicky and Jeff and Tony and Sue all got along rather well. They had been out for a couple of pub lunches and the ladies spoke on the phone. There was something about being at a séance that bonded people.

Judy had been quite a sensation amongst the medium community. The tape recording of the séance had been transmitted around the world with her description of the story leading up to the evening and the events that occurred. She was travelling to America, soon, to give a number of talks on the subject.

Iris bought a small, leatherbound journal and made her notes about Harold and the curse. She added her volume to the ones Mabel had written and then they were put into an antique display cabinet, which she had got from a junk shop and painstakingly restored. The photograph album had been redone, too, and the pictures had been put online to preserve them.

Mel and Ian had got engaged, much to everyone's excitement. All of the people from the séance would be on the guest list for the wedding and it would be an opportunity to catch up. They didn't talk a great deal about what had happened that evening, they were all moving on with their lives.

Hugh Forsyth didn't really make much of effort to see his daughter. Iris was not really disappointed. He had told his sons about their half-sister and she had met them. They were the first to say that their father was lovable, but unreliable. She had seen him and that was enough for her.

What had happened to Harold? Iris had wondered many times about where he had gone. Was he in purgatory, or hell, or nowhere, his atoms scattered into the ether. Mabel had told them that he was gone and that was sufficient.

Iris would have loved to speak to her mother. Not questions about what she did and why. She wanted to tell her that she was happy. The, substitute parents had been wonderful and now she had got to know her grandmother, as well. Mike and her had Edward, and would, hopefully, have another child. Family life was good for them.